MY BEST DECISION

SARA'S STORY

CAROLE WOLFE

BLIND VISTA PRESS

COPYRIGHT

Copyright © 2020 Carole Wolfe

All rights reserved.

www.carolewolfe.com

First Edition

ISBN 978-0-9993582-4-5 (EPUB edition)
ISBN 978-0-9993582-5-2 (Paperback edition)
ISBN 978-0-9993582-6-9 (Large print paperback edition)

This is a work of fiction. Names, characters, businesses, places, events, locales, and incidents are either the products of the author's imagination or used in a fictitious manner. Any resemblance to actual persons, living or dead, or actual events is purely coincidental.

1

Sara checked the last item off her to-do list. She placed her pen in its rightful home, the "World's Best Aunt" mug her niece and nephew gave her for her birthday last year. Sitting back in her chair, Sara glanced around her office. Stacks of neatly organized folders waited to be returned to the file room. The stack was shorter than the previous year when her partners refused to convert anything to a digital format. She'd managed to get all the new incoming cases onto the law firm's intranet, but they still dealt with the paper files on the older cases.

The last few months had been quiet. Almost too quiet. She was used to dealing with her sister's ridiculous legal issues, but since Tasha's ex-husband left town, things had been calm. No yelling sprees. No odd business proposals. No drunken accidents. The cases she worked had been a pain, though.

After months of negotiating, the dog custody case was almost finished. Why people argued over a dog was beyond her, but Sara had grown to love him. Tiny, a 225-pound St. Bernard, calmed her down whenever he came with his owner to a meeting. The animal himself was a nervous wreck, but his presence in the office would be missed by everyone. Everyone except for Renee, of course. The firm's receptionist ended up on dog clean-up duty on more than one occasion.

There was a knock at the door and Sara called out, "Come in."

As if her thoughts had drawn her in, Renee opened the door and walked into the room. She headed straight to the pile of files and tapped them.

"Right on schedule," Renee said as she headed back to the door. "Do you need anything else from me tonight? I've got roller derby practice and need to get home to change before I head to the rink."

"How do you do that?" Sara tilted her head to the side. "You always come in right as I'm finishing up."

"You are regular as clockwork, Sara," said Renee. She winked at her boss. "Plus, I can see your to-do list from my computer."

Sara laughed at her oversight before saying, "Tiny's case file is in there. I'm waiting on a response from the attorney, but I think we're almost there. Will you be sad to see Tiny go?"

"No!" the receptionist complained. "That animal has the tiniest bladder ever!"

"Not true. I've seen how many paper towels it takes for you to clean up after him," said Sara, stifling a smile. "Looks like about a gallon of liquid every time."

Renee scowled at her boss.

"Fine. Most overactive bladder. You wouldn't think this was funny if you had to clean up after him."

Sara shrugged as she said, "You got the better end of the deal."

The scowl was replaced by a frown.

"Why do you say that?"

"The dog is pretty nice, aside from peeing in the office when he got nervous. His owners, on the other hand, have a nasty bark and bite," said Sara. "I know cleaning up after Tiny isn't what you signed up to do here, but I appreciate it. We all do. I'm sure Rich and Bill would agree."

Sara doubted her law firm partners would ever share their appreciation with Renee, but the compliment mollified Renee.

"Thanks. It's nice to hear that now and then," said Renee. She flashed a wicked smile. "So, since you seem to be in a benevolent mood, can I ask for some time off?"

Sara pulled up her calendar on her computer.

"I suppose you can make a request. What days do you need?"

Despite being the first and only female partner at Smith, Rogers & Shaw, LLC, general administrative and HR responsibilities landed on her desk. She'd gotten used to it and as Renee was the only employee, it was easy. Since Renee was only going to be off for a few days, the office would survive. If she needed to, Sara could make a quick call to the temp agency for an extra hand.

After she put Renee's request into her calendar, they reviewed tomorrow's schedule. The business review meeting with Carlton Reynolds made her grin. At first, Sara thought it would be awkward to work with the chiropractor considering she'd once had a secret crush on him. They'd gone to the same yoga studio a while ago and Sara'd been working up the courage to ask him out when she discovered he was dating Brad Gerome, her ex-brother-in-law's brother. She'd hesitated to work with him when he asked for advice on his business, but it turned out to be a good thing. He was the perfect client and had become a great friend. It also helped that Brad still kept in touch with Tasha and babysat her niece and nephew on occasion.

Sara also noticed a meeting with the owner of the local diner, Betty's Coffee Bar.

"What do you suppose she wants this time?" Renee asked as she picked up the files from Sara's desk. "Is she still mad about the softball uniforms? Personally, I think they look cute."

Sara shook her head.

"I warned Betty." Sara'd negotiated a truce between Tasha and Betty a few months before. Betty agreed to keep Tasha's personal problems to herself instead of telling every customer she got through the doors of the cafe and Tasha would purchase new uniforms for her softball team. "She should've picked out exactly what she wanted, rather than giving Tasha full control. Now the team's stuck with those pink skorts for a few years."

"Okay, I'm out of here," said Renee. "I'll see you in the morning."

Sara stretched her arms over her head.

"Goodnight. I'm leaving soon, too."

"Heading to the new yoga class?" asked Renee, smiling as Sara frowned at her. "You haven't been going to the one with Dr. Reynolds lately."

Sara told Renee what she told anyone who asked.

"I'm trying out a new style. Hot yoga is great but I'm ready for a change."

Renee winked at her.

"And I hear the instructor is handsome, too. That can't hurt either." Without waiting for a response, Renee skipped out the door with the files.

Wondering why a grown woman would skip, Sara logged out of her laptop and put it in her briefcase. She tucked a few files in as well so she could review them later. Pushing back from her desk, she sighed. Changing yoga studios hadn't helped fill the void in her dating life. She'd hoped to meet someone there, but the only thing she found was improved flexibility.

Sara didn't care so much about her lack of good dating material, but her mother continued to pester her. For some reason, Sara had assumed when she returned to her hometown after law school and took a job with a local firm, her mother would deem her a success. She should have known better. Despite all of her accomplishments professionally, Helene found fault in Sara's lack of a significant other.

She shook her head when she remembered how she'd narrowly escaped a speed dating session. Her sister ended up going twice and Sara had laughed at her for falling into her mother's trap, but she found herself dodging the problem now.

Grabbing her bag, Sara walked to the door and turned off her office light. She looked back inside and thought about how her family and a few friends had sat in this room a few months back. She liked to keep her work and personal life separate, but things were changing. Ever since Tasha had stood up to her ex-husband, the sisters had spent more time doing fun things together instead of dealing with silly legal problems. Sara hoped that Tasha had outgrown her need for drama because it was nice to just hang out.

She headed down the hall and poked her head into Rich's office. Her partner's desk was covered in papers, and rap music blared from his computer. Sara waved her arms in the air to catch his attention, and he turned down the volume to what she considered a dull roar.

"How can you concentrate with that stuff on?" she asked for the umpteenth time. "Silence is golden."

"Each to his own. I can't stand that gong crap you play when you're working." Rich leaned back in his chair and put his hands behind his head. "Heading out for the night?"

She nodded.

"Renee asked off next week. I marked it on the firm calendar." She waved as she turned to go. "Goodnight."

"Wait!" Rich called before she could move. "I have trial prep next week. I'm going to need someone full time."

Sara frowned.

"There isn't a case on the calendar. I checked before I gave her the time off."

Rich glanced at her sheepishly. She was glad she worked with him and not dated him. The man used his sad puppy-dog eyes to manipulate women, clients, and even judges to get what he wanted.

Not going to work on me, thought Sara.

"I forgot to ask Renee to put it in the calendar," he said. He ran his hands through his hair. "Even so, I'm surprised you gave her the time off considering Doug's big announcement. Tasha has to be freaking out by now."

The hair on her arms stood at attention at the sound of her ex-brother-in-law's name.

"What are you talking about?"

"Hang on," Rich said, pushing papers around his messy desk. "I have the article here somewhere."

She stepped into the office. If Rich's desk was as disorganized as usual, he would need her help to find what he was looking for.

Before she could assist, Rich lifted a folded newspaper above his head.

"Here it is!"

"You know you can read that online and not get newsprint on your hands," said Sara.

He handed the paper to her and she took it gingerly.

"I'm old school. What can I say?"

Sara turned to walk out of the office when Rich said, "No, stay here and read it. I want to see your reaction."

Letting out a sigh of frustration, Sara leaned against the wall and glanced down at the headline.

"Prodigal son promises to revitalize riverfront building"

Feeling the energy drain out of her, Sara hobbled to the chair.

"Is this as bad as it sounds?" asked Sara.

"Worse," replied Rich. "Keep reading."

2

Sinking into the chair, Sara closed her eyes and took a deep, cleansing breath. Whatever was in the newspaper article was not unbearable or insurmountable. Doug the Douche, her nickname for her ex-brother-in-law, couldn't cause any more problems for her or her family.

If I repeat this enough, it will work, she thought.

Or she could open her eyes and face this challenge like the attorney she was.

Sitting up straight, Sara opened her eyes and read the article.

"Prodigal son promises to revitalize riverfront buildings"
By Cynthia Anderson
Gazette reporter

FORMER RESIDENT DOUG GEROME announced he will head up the renovation of several buildings in the riverfront area. Gerome, who currently resides in Saint Thomas VI, told the Gazette work is underway to obtain the necessary permits and permissions to remodel the buildings. In his application paperwork, Gerome stated the dilapidated conditions of the area encouraged vagrants to congregate there, leading to an increase in crime and drug use.

"Renovation of these buildings promises affordable housing as well as an entertainment hub to draw visitors to the area," said Gerome in his application. "Who better than someone with first-hand knowledge of the community to bring the opportunity to its citizens."

Newly elected Mayor Nicole Pilchard placed the request on the agenda for the next city council meeting, which is scheduled for the last Monday of the month.

Pilchard shared some of Gerome's proposal with The Gazette.

"In addition to cost-effective apartments, the plan includes space for casual and upscale dining establishments, an office share complex, retail space, as well as an indoor inflatable center and trampoline park," said Pilchard. "This type of venture promotes productive use of a run-down and underused area."

The project is reportedly being financed by The Miller Agency. The Gazette attempted to contact the group but its attorney, Jared Hughes, declined comment.

Disclosure: The Gazette previously reported that Gerome was injured in a single car collision earlier this year. An investigation into the crash found that an equipment failure caused the crash and no charges were filed against Gerome.

"He did it again." Sara dropped the newspaper on the corner of Rich's desk. "How can anyone believe a word from that man? Has he not shown his true colors?"

Rich tucked his hands behind his head and leaned back in his chair.

"You're taking this better than I expected. I thought there would be screaming and cursing."

Sara stood up and paced around Rich's office.

"I'm far too disciplined for that. Why scream and curse when it won't fix anything?" She pointed her index finger at Rich as his mouth opened. "Besides, I should be cussing you out. I have to call the temp agency tomorrow because of you."

Rich picked up the newspaper and spread it out on his desk.

"What are you going to tell your sister?"

She shrugged.

"Nothing. I'm sure my mother has already heard about it. She can break the news to Tasha." Sara picked up her briefcase and headed to the door. "We all know how much my mother loves sharing news with people."

"That's it?" Rich called out after her. "You're not even going to speculate how he avoided charges?"

Resting her head on the doorjamb, Sara looked back at her partner. She knew Cynthia would never have added that disclosure if it wasn't true. The reporter was thorough, and she didn't believe in gray areas. Rich must have caught wind of something juicy, or he wouldn't have mentioned it. She didn't care what her ex-brother-in-law was doing, but her legal mind was curious how a cut and dried case got thrown out. The police charged Doug with a DUI after he crashed his rental car into a tree while being intoxicated. Someone must have pulled some strings to get something like that dropped.

"Okay. I'll take the bait," said Sara. "You obviously know how Doug got out of it. Spill."

A satisfied smile passed over Rich's face.

"I thought you'd never ask." He pointed at the newspaper. "You know the attorney who didn't want to comment?"

"Jared Hughes? I've never heard of him." she asked.

"Where have you been? Hughes is only the preeminent land use and zoning lawyer in the Midwest who also happens to be a college football legend. His stats were phenomenal. I think he set some records that still stand."

Refraining from asking why football statistics were relevant, Sara asked, "Okay. He's an attorney. So am I. What's the big deal?"

"The big deal is that everything the man touches turns to gold."

"Then why would this guy put Doug Gerome in charge of it?" Sara didn't understand. "A man who cheated on his wife, denied paternity of his children and wrapped a rental car around a tree?"

Rich frowned. "When you put it like that, it doesn't make sense. But, rumor has it that when Hughes picked Doug for the project, the DUI charges were dropped. You know how much our judge loves his college football."

Skeptical, Sara tilted her head and frowned.

"How exactly did you get that information?"

Rich mimicked zipping his mouth shut, twisting a key, and throwing the imaginary key over his shoulder.

"You're no help at all," said Sara as she turned to the door. A sudden flare of temper caused her to turn back. "If this man has any sense of propriety, he would run as fast as he could from Doug. It doesn't take much to figure out what an ass Doug is."

"True," said Rich. He stood up and walked over to where Sara stood, leaned against the wall, and crossed his arms. "But remember, Doug's great at manipulating people. You and I both know that."

Shaking her head, Sara shifted her briefcase to the other shoulder.

"Yes, we do. And while I appreciate you getting me up to speed, I'm not getting in the middle of this. Tasha can hear about it on her own. If I tell her, she's going to assume I'm worried about it. And I'm not."

"Your mother's going to tell her, and you are worried about

her. She's your sister," said Rich as he started back to his desk. As he sat down, he smiled over at Sara. "Don't forget the temp I need next week."

Shaking her head, Sara walked out of the room and headed to the lobby, the conversation about Doug replaying in her head. There wasn't anything she could do about it, but she knew it wasn't a good thing to have Doug back in town. Since he left, she'd seen Tasha's life blossom. Her sister was more comfortable in her own skin and had started dating again. Her niece and nephew seemed happier as well.

She didn't want to get involved with this, but maybe it wouldn't hurt if she did some digging to find out what Doug was really up to. After all, she didn't want her family in danger again.

Jared Hughes may need to be educated about what Doug was really like.

3

The next morning Sara cradled her chin in her hand. She'd been on hold with the Orion Temp Agency for twenty minutes. In that time, she'd memorized the company's mission statement and knew it only used bonded and insured employees. If she didn't have a contract in place with them, she would've already hung up.

While she waited, Sara skimmed the website of The Miller Agency. Well designed and flashy, it skimped on details. From what she read, the agency specialized in buying underutilized buildings and renovating them. It sounded like the home makeover show her sister watched, except for commercial buildings. Jared Hughes was the only person named on the website, and his biography restated what Rich already told her.

An Ivy League undergraduate, Jared led his team to three consecutive winning seasons and still held the record for the most completed passes. His law school days boasted head of Law Review and top of his class.

"Maybe he had too many concussions and that's why he hired Doug." Sara shook her head. She knew it wasn't fair to judge people like that, but still, some people had to work hard for what they got. From what she read Jared Hughes came about things easily. At least the way it appeared he did.

The hold music discontinued when a woman spoke.

"Sorry for the wait. This is Laura. How can I help you?"

"Yes, this is Sara Shaw at Smith, Rogers & Shaw. We have a contract with you for temp services on an ad hoc basis. I need a receptionist for next week. Our requirements are in our file." She leaned back in the chair, thankful to have someone real to speak with.

"Oh. Well. Now, I'm new here so you're gonna have to bear with me for a bit," Laura said. Sara thought the woman sounded breathless. "Can you say all that again? But slowly."

Resting her head on her hand, Sara asked, "Is Claudia available? She's my account rep. I'm sure she can get this taken care without having to bother you."

"No, ma'am. Claudia is no longer with us. Just little old me. Laura. I'll be working with you going forward." Sara heard another phone ring in the background and Laura said, "Can you hold please? I have to get that."

Before Sara could protest, hold music filled her ears. Groaning, Sara wished she could call another temp agency. But part of living in a small town meant her choices were limited, so she turned her gaze back to her computer while she waited.

If The Miller Agency website wouldn't reveal anything, then she needed to do some Internet research. It appeared she had plenty of time while she was on hold for Laura.

"Claudia never made me wait," she said to herself as she began typing. After a few searches, Sara saw a familiar name. Ron Walters, Doug's former divorce attorney, was the local contact for the renovation. Having Doug employed and making money would be a plus for Ron. Sara remembered Ron mentioning a while back that Doug was behind on paying his bills.

Sitting back in her chair, Sara thought about what she knew

of Ron. He was a decent general attorney, although he failed to win any cases for Doug. Sara knew the failure was due to Ron's uncooperative client, so she couldn't hold that against him. What didn't make sense was why he would hire a client to work for him? Especially a client who didn't pay his bills. Maybe this was Ron's way of recouping his money?

"Okay, I'm back. Now you said you needed some help next week. Tell me again your name."

Struggling to maintain her cool, Sara said, "Sara Shaw at Smith, Rogers & Shaw. We're a law firm. We need a temp for next week."

"There's no need to get snappy, ma'am. I'm doing the best I can."

Irritated her impatience showed, Sara stood up and paced. It wasn't going to make anything easier if this woman hung up on her. Maybe she needed a vacation.

"Okay, I've got your account pulled up. Admin. Receptionist. Light filing," said Laura. "You know, there's no mention of legal experience required. Why isn't that in your profile?"

"I don't know. Claudia knew what we needed, so I assumed it was in the file." Hoping to avoid any more questions from Laura, Sara said, "As long as you have someone who can answer the phones and deal with clients coming into the office, we should be fine."

"Will they have to serve coffee and snacks?"

Sara scrunched her face up as a silent scream worked its way out of her system.

"Yes, they'll need to offer coffee and snacks."

The line fell silent, only the clicking of the computer keyboard making its presence known. Sara steeled herself for the wait. At least the woman was attempting to find someone.

Just when she thought it was a lost cause, Laura said, "You are in luck. I have a new temp starting work on Monday. She can do her new employee training and then I'll send her straight over."

Resigned that was the best she was going to get Sara thanked Laura and requested the necessary information be emailed to her. It shouldn't be too hard to teach someone how to answer the phones for a few days. She hoped.

Pleased she got something checked off her list, Sara hung up and turned back to her computer. She'd found the connection between Doug and Hughes, but she needed to figure out what to do with it. Before she could do any more research, a reminder message popped up on her screen.

Carlton would be here soon to review his business documents. She'd already gone through them and had a list of things that needed to be revised or amended. In her typical efficient fashion, the list was organized by necessity: Required, Recommended, and Optional. All that needed to be done was talk to Carlton and see if he was amenable.

The phone rang. Assuming it was Renee letting her know Carlton arrived, she grabbed it without checking caller ID.

"Sara Shaw."

"Have you been so busy you couldn't trouble yourself to call me and let me know my ex-son-in-law is back in town?" Sara pulled the phone away from her ear as her mother's voice screeched over the line. "Is it asking too much to be informed by my own daughter? I had to find out at Betty's Coffee Bar of all places."

"Mother, you find everything out at Betty's. Why would this be any different?" She was surprised at her mother's reaction. Helene got most of her news in gossip form, so why this tidbit bothered her, Sara didn't know. "Doug is Tasha's ex-husband, not mine. Shouldn't she be the one to inform you of these things?"

Sara imagined the look of irritation she knew was plastered on her mother's face.

"That's not the point. You're more on top of the news than your sister. I'd expect you would want to stay in the loop. Especially since there's going to be an influx of businesses in town. It could mean new clients for you, right?"

Sara said, "I think you're getting ahead of yourself. This is a renovation project on a few buildings down by the riverfront. The Miller Agency is probably bringing in its own contractors. Not sure that will affect me."

"Ah ha! So, you did know about it and kept it from me."

Sara's line beeped, signaling another call coming in. Jumping on the opportunity, she said to her mother, "I'm on my way to a client meeting, Mom. I'll have to call you back later."

"Then why did you answer when I called, young lady?"

Leaning her forehead into her empty palm and squeezing her eyes closed, Sara said, "Honestly, I thought you were Renee telling me Carlton was here."

Her mother's tone of voice changed instantly.

"Dr. Reynolds is there? Well, why didn't you say so? What a sweet man. Don't keep him waiting. That's rude, and I raised you better than that. Be sure to tell him I said hello. Oh, make sure he tells Brad hi for me, too! But don't think this conversation is finished. You know better than to keep big news like this from me. I have a reputation to uphold."

The dial tone buzzing in her ear indicated the call was over and Sara let out a breath of air as she hung up the phone.

Why didn't I move away after law school?

The phone rang again, and she picked it back up.

"Dr. Reynolds is here," said Renee. "Do you want me to show him to your office?"

"Can you show him to the conference room please? I'll meet you there."

Without waiting for Renee's response, she hung up the phone and stood. Conversations with her mother always left her tense and anxious and that was no way to go into a client meeting, even a routine meeting like this one. Knowing some quick yoga would help, Sara carefully took off her high heels. She placed them neatly beside her desk and stood in mountain pose. Bringing her leg up into tree pose, she took a deep breath and closed her eyes. The irritation of talking with her mother slowly drained from her body, and she felt an energizing force replace the frustration. After another quick breath, she put her foot back on the ground and opened her eyes. Gone was the browbeaten daughter. Back was the kick-ass attorney. Sara stepped into her shoes, grabbed her laptop and files and headed to the conference room.

4

Tasha finished typing out the report. As a member of the Welcoming Committee at her kids' school, she submitted a summary of who she talked to each month. It was nice to meet new parents, but she hadn't counted on the reports. The president of the PTO had turned out to be a micromanager and wanted things done a certain way.

"At least I'm not on the Fundraising Committee," she said to herself. "I'd die listening to the pros and cons of cookie dough."

She proofread the report, emailed it to the president, then smiled as she looked around her spotless living room. Not for the first time, Tasha shook her head in amazement. It had taken a lifetime, but she'd finally got a handle on how to keep her house clean. Ever since she told her ex-husband she was finished putting up with his crap, things had changed. On the other hand, she might just have got sick of living in a disorganized mess. Either way, she enjoyed relaxing in a chaos-free zone.

Focusing back on her computer, she pulled up her email and began parsing through it. Advertisements were deleted immediately as were the phishing and junk email. She hovered her cursor over an email from *The Gazette* and was getting ready to delete it when something caught her attention. Tasha pulled up the email to see what it was about.

She knew that not so long ago, the headline she was reading would have spun her out of control. Her ex-husband had had that effect on her for years, but ever since she'd confronted him, Tasha felt free. She knew she should've done it years ago, but timing was everything.

She clicked on the link in the email that lead to a sparse newspaper article telling her one thing: Doug was back in town. Tasha waited to see how she felt about it. Her body didn't react. Her stomach felt fine and her muscles remained relaxed. She didn't care. He wasn't her problem anymore. She moved on to the next email, which did interest her. The email from Greg made her smile in anticipation.

Hi! I didn't need anything. I wanted to tell you I had a great time with you and the kids bowling last weekend. Do you think they would want to go ice skating? We could give that a try. Let me know and I'll check out the public skate times.

Also, would you like to go to dinner on Saturday night? My mom offered to babysit for us. I could get reservations at the Italian place you like.

Have a great day!

The thought of spending more time with Greg warmed her heart. They'd been going out regularly for the last couple of months, both as a couple and with the kids, but they hadn't had *The Conversation* yet. Were they friends? Were they a couple? Did they have a future together?

"Friends don't kiss like that though," Tasha said to the empty living room. Her cheeks flamed up thinking about how she felt after spending time with Greg. Giddy, silly, and excited summed it up. She relaxed back into the couch and reflected on the situation. Despite being married before, she couldn't remember feeling this way. Tasha was far more optimistic about Greg than she ever was about Doug. It didn't make sense, especially since she experienced firsthand that relationships don't always turn out the way you plan. For some reason, she thought she would be leery of her feelings the second time around. Sure, she'd been younger before and fell in love without understanding the consequences. Getting married the first time was an adventure. She didn't know what a mess she would end up in. She shook her head as she thought about all the other factors in her failed marriage.

She wondered if the $116 million lottery windfall she and Doug hit was the beginning of the end of the marriage or if it would've imploded, anyway? Reaching for her cup of tea, she remembered how her sister warned her early on that Doug was no good. He'd made a pass at her right before the wedding, but Tasha hadn't believed Sara. Too bad she hadn't. It would've saved her a lot of drama.

Thinking of Sara, Tasha wondered how she was doing. They'd spent a lot of time together lately, and Sara supported her new relationship with Greg. In fact, she encouraged it, perhaps too much. Every time Tasha brought up Sara's love life, her sister changed the subject back to Greg.

Tasha would have done the same thing in her sister's position. Having a crush on a gay man who happened to be in a relationship with a friend would embarrass anyone. Sara brushed off the incident, but Tasha knew the revelation took its toll.

At least Mom didn't find out, Tasha thought, putting her tea on the side table. She focused back on the computer. *Enough about Sara. Let's focus on my love life.*

She tapped out a sweet, yet not sappy reply to Greg and sent it before cleaning out the rest of her email. After a few minutes, the only ones left were the one from Greg and the one from *The Gazette*. She was about to delete the email from the newspaper but stopped.

Does Sara know about this? Does she need to? Tasha thought as she sipped the rest of her tea. She looked at the tea leaves in the bottom of her cup as she made a decision. *Forewarned is forearmed.*

With that in mind, Tasha put the cup back on the table and forwarded the email to her sister. She took a quick glance at her daily schedule to see what else she needed to accomplish before the kids got home from school. One task was to run to Betty's Coffee Bar to pick up the pie that Blake and Libby had requested for dessert. While her baking skills were getting better, nothing beat Betty's cherry pie. She had a few other odds and ends to grab so she shut her laptop and headed to get her purse, pushing all thoughts of her idiot ex-husband out of her head.

5

Sara walked down the short hallway from her office to the conference room where Carlton was waiting. Voices drifted out of the room, and Sara stopped when she heard her name.

"So, do you know why Sara switched yoga studios?"

The question irritated her. Her partner, Bill Smith, shouldn't be asking her client about her personal life. She knew he meant well, but she needed to talk to him about boundaries. Just because she was the newest member of the firm and he was old enough to be her father, didn't give him the right to pry.

Carlton answered before she could enter the room. "You have to make changes sometimes. I'm sure she just wanted something new."

Pleased with Carlton's response, Sara walked in.

"Good morning, Carlton," she said as she extended her hand to shake her client's. "Sorry to keep you waiting." She nodded at Bill. "Thanks for keeping him company. I'll take over from here."

Bill had the decency to look down at his feet as he walked out the door. Sara followed and closed the door behind him.

"You heard Bill ask about yoga, didn't you?" Carlton settled down in a chair. "You handled it well. I wouldn't have been so nice if someone was snooping in my life."

Shaking her head, Sara said, "Sadly, I'm getting used to it. Everyone wants to get involved in my life for some reason. Never expected my business partners to interfere though."

Sara opened her laptop to get started, but a knock at the door interrupted them.

"Yes," she said as Renee poked her head round the door. "We're just starting our meeting. What can I help you with?"

Renee shook her head and smiled at Carlton instead.

"Can I get you anything to drink? I should have offered you coffee or water. I'm not sure what's gotten into me today."

Observing the way Renee ogled at Carlton, Sara knew exactly what had gotten into her receptionist. Renee had a fondness for cute men, and despite the fact she knew Brad and Carlton were together, it was typical of Renee to stop in for another look.

Add "discuss professionalism with Renee" to my to-do list, thought Sara.

"No, thank you," Carlton said. "I'm fine."

"Well, if you need anything, just call." She wiggled her fingers toward the phone before she left the room, the door closing behind her.

"Wow, was it me or did she come across a bit flirty when she asked for my drink order?" Carlton asked.

Rolling her eyes, Sara said, "Sorry about that. I'll have a chat with her. She's in vacation mode. Next week, she's taking some time off."

"No problem from my part." Carlton nodded toward Sara's computer. "So, what do you have for me?"

The meeting didn't take long. It was helpful to have a client who paid attention to his own business. She handed him a sheet of paper, summarizing their conversation, the issues and how to fix everything.

"That was the most efficient meeting I've ever had," Carlton said as he tucked the sheet in his portfolio. "Are you sure that's it? I feel like this should have taken longer."

"As someone who bills by the hour, my partners think I should slow down a bit," Sara admitted. "I could handle all this for you, but you can do most of the work yourself and save the fees. I'm happy to do a final review of the documents before you put them into use. It shouldn't take more than an hour to go over the files again."

"Thanks for helping me with these. I'm glad I took Brad's advice to work with you."

"Me too," Sara said as she gathered up her computer and stood.

"How is Brad? I haven't seen him for a while." They walked toward the door. "You two must be busy."

"We've been swamped. The hospital project is in its final stages, and he started another building. And as you can see," he pointed to his portfolio, "my business is going pretty well too. Hey, you should join us for taco night sometime. Libby and Blake love a good fish taco."

Sara laughed. "That's right. You're the one who introduced the taco holders shaped like dinosaurs! Blake loved those so much he asked me to get some for my house. Where did you find them?"

"A client of mine gave me a set so I got them out for the kids to try. I wanted to send them home with Blake and Libby, but Tasha wouldn't let me. She thought it would be more fun for them to come to our house and have dinner with a triceratops and a brontosaurus."

"I'll have to keep looking around then," said Sara. "I found a baking mold for pigs in a blanket that Blake likes, but he still asks for the taco holders."

Smiling at the pig reference, Carlton asked, "What is it about pigs and your family? I vividly recall Tasha's oinking pig slippers from her time in my office."

"Yeah, those things set off quite the chain of events, didn't they?"

Sara led Carlton out to the lobby. She frowned when she noticed Renee staring at Carlton but before she could say anything, the phone rang, and Renee answered it.

"It was an interesting time for sure," she said. Waving goodbye, she headed back to her office.

6

Dropping into her chair, Sara put her head into her hands and sighed. Bill's nosiness had to stop. While Sara knew he meant well, asking a client about her personal life was inappropriate. Come to think of it, Rich's assumption that she would be his administrative assistant while Renee was on vacation wasn't good either. Her partners didn't take her seriously and she needed to put her foot down. And speaking of Renee, she needed to address proper etiquette with clients.

"How do I tactfully tell them," she mumbled to herself, "to keep your eyes on your own business?"

"Problems with your mother again?" asked a voice from the hallway.

Sara's head whipped up to see Bill standing in her doorway.

"No." Sara considered addressing Bill's nosiness. She liked having a plan in place before confronting people, especially when those people were her counterparts. Making a mental note to decide how to handle Bill, Sara sat back in her chair and crossed her arms. "What can I help you with?"

When Bill's eyes narrowed in concentration, she knew he didn't believe her.

"You haven't been yourself for a while, Sara. What's going on?"

Not now, she thought. She felt her shoulders crawl up toward her ears in her irritation, and she forced them back down. Letting Bill get to her wasn't the solution. She gave Bill a smile.

"Same as always. Lots of work going on. My own, plus Renee is out next week and Rich has a trial. I've had to spend some time finding a temp." When Bill opened his mouth to speak, Sara put her hand up and stopped him. "But don't worry. Everything is under control. The agency is sending someone over on Monday. I can handle it."

"I'm sure you can. You always do," said Bill as he walked into her office and put his hands on the back of her side chair. "But you seem worked up. You okay?"

If you'd stop asking me stupid questions, I'd be fine, she thought. Willing herself to relax, Sara pushed the files around on her desk, searching for a viable explanation that didn't involve accusing Bill of being a busybody like her mother. When nothing occurred to her, she changed tactics.

"Did you need something? If not, I have work to do." She nodded down at her desk. Sara sounded rude, even to herself, but the last thing she wanted was her partner delving into her personal life.

"Sara, I don't want to tell you what to do, but you need to relax a little. You're an asset to the firm, but I'm wondering now if you're spread too thin." Bill walked back to the doorway, nodding to himself the entire time. "Maybe you shouldn't have given Renee time off."

Her temper flared as Bill continued, "Or better yet, maybe we should get some more help." Bill scratched his head, reminding Sara of Tiny when he scratched his ears. The comparison of her partner to a dog wasn't flattering, but Bill's condescending behavior irked her. Biting her tongue, she remained silent as he continued, "Yes, it makes sense. Business is good. Calendars are full. I'll add it to the agenda for the next partner's meeting. We'll need your help to find candidates, but once we get someone hired, you should have less to do. How does that sound?"

Rather than share her frustration, Sara nodded.

"Sure. Perhaps the temp they send next week would work."

Bill nodded and walked into the hallway.

"In the meantime, relax. You're doing a great job."

She waited until Bill's footsteps faded away before she flipped him off and turned to her computer. She should have nipped Bill's behavior in the bud. It will be that much harder now that she let him off the hook this time.

A *ping* sounded, alerting her to an incoming email. *On to the next distraction*, thought Sara as she pulled up her messages and scrolled through them. She opened the one from her sister first, expecting to read a panicked missive about Doug showing up in town. A hint of excitement dashed through her as she prepared to talk her sister off the figurative ledge. It would be nice to be in control after listening to Bill's little speech. The excitement vanished though when she read her sister's brief email:

FYI. Thought you should know. Have a great day! :)

Sara stared at the screen for a few seconds while she pondered her sister's response. Apparently, Tasha's transformation was complete. Doug no longer affected her.

There's hope for me yet. If Doug the Douche has lost his power, then I'll be able to put my partners and mother in their rightful places.

Realizing her job was done as far as her sister was concerned, she moved to the next email.

Why would Cynthia Anderson from The Gazette be emailing me?

Sara wasn't involved in anything Cynthia reported on, nor

did Sara have any clients who had been in the news lately. She clicked on the email and began reading. It didn't take long to figure out what Cynthia wanted.

Doug.

Cynthia's email stated that she was doing some additional investigating into Doug's accident. The circumstances of the dismissal of the case seemed odd to her and she wanted to know if Sara could give any further details.

Shaking her head, Sara turned to her Zen sand garden. She picked up the miniature rake and made straight lines in the sand. This was her favorite gift from her niece and nephew, and it helped settle her mind, which always seemed in need of calming these days. As she made patterns in the sand, she considered the reporter's email. It's not like Sara could comment on the DUI case. She didn't have any specifics, and speculation wasn't her thing. It didn't make sense why Cynthia would reach out to her.

Sara considered her next move. Ignoring the email made the most sense, but she decided to loop Bill and Rich in on the situation, should Cynthia complain to them. Experience taught her that Cynthia didn't like to be ignored. Sara dropped the rake in the sand garden and forwarded the message on to her partners. One more reason to have a sit down with her partners. She needed to explain that even though she was the most recent partner, she was still an equal partner.

Staring at the neat lines in the sand garden, Sara thought about why Cynthia might be snooping around. She grabbed a legal pad and her favorite pen. Computers were great for some things, but Sara preferred to do her brainstorming on paper.

Her neat handwriting soon filled the page with all the players: The Miller Agency, Jared Hughes, Ron Walters, and Doug Gerome. The links to the players were there but the reasoning behind them wasn't as obvious. Rich had been vague with his details, but he knew something, which meant there was something to find in this mess.

Tapping the pen on her chin, she decided the easiest thing to do would be call Ron. They'd talked before and despite his poor choice of clients, Ron was a decent attorney.

Twenty minutes later, Sara put the phone down and pushed away from her desk. She shook her head as if that would clear out the ridiculous story she'd just heard. Knowing that it wouldn't, she grabbed her purse. She rarely took a break for lunch, but today she was going to make an exception. Maybe a change of scenery would give her an idea about what to do next.

7

Sara zipped out into the lobby and gave Renee a quick wave.

"I'll be back later. I'm going to lunch."

Without waiting for a response, she left Renee open-mouthed in the office and headed straight to her reliable sedan. It stood out like a sore thumb between the luxury SUV Bill drove and Rich's sporty convertible. Her partners made fun of her conservative approach to transportation, but she didn't see the point of spending a lot of money on an expensive car that required more money for upkeep. She'd rather spend her hard-earned cash on important things, like clothes and shoes. A quick glance down at her black patent leather heels made her smile.

Now these were a great buy!

Sara slid behind the wheel and sat there while she decided where to go. Her usual green salad with extra veggies, no dressing and tofu didn't appeal to her. She wanted something different, so she took off toward Betty's Coffee Bar. A comfort meal of a macaroni and cheese would hit the spot. Plus, the drive would give her some time to put all the facts together.

Pulling out of the parking lot, Sara thought about what she learned from Ron.

The attorney confirmed what Rich hinted at: Ron had been asked to find someone local to be the spokesperson for the renovation but who met certain expectations. While she couldn't get the exact parameters out of Ron, he did say Doug was the only person he knew who met The Miller Agency's specifications. Sara also confirmed Rich's assertion that sports had something to do with Doug's DUI charge being dismissed.

"That's attorney-client privilege. But did you know Jared Hughes was the winningest quarterback in the Ivy League? Ever? You know how big football is around here. It can move mountains," Ron had said before changing the subject. "By the way, is Tasha really paying Doug's bills again? He told me to send his past-due statements to her."

Sara chuckled at her suggestion of what Ron could do with his statements as she continued down the street, noticing what a nice day it was. While she usually preferred to place her order to go, so she could eat in the privacy of her office, a picnic in the park sounded like a better idea. Sitting outside might help her process her current situation.

She pulled into the parking lot and saw her sister's minivan near the entrance of Betty's. Pleased with the coincidence, she parked her car and headed into the store. It was such a nice day that the door was propped open and Sara heard the argument that was in progress.

"I can't believe I let you order those ridiculous uniforms for the softball team. Those stupid skorts are a pain in the butt." Betty's deep booming voice drifted out of the coffee shop. "My catcher can't even squat without the ruffle getting caught in her chest protector."

Sara poked her head in the store to see what was happening. Her sister perused the glass front pastry display with a grin plastered on her face.

"I figured the leg guards would be more of a problem," said Tasha. "An issue with the chest protector never crossed my mind. Maybe next time you should be more specific when you bribe me for uniforms."

Betty's hand smacked down on the countertop.

"I knew it. You're trying to make us the laughingstock of the league. Tanking my reputation is one thing but messing with my team's ability to play the game is another. And let me remind you, if your mother hadn't blabbed in the first place, this never would've happened."

Wondering if she should speak up to help her sister or let the situation continue, Sara got her answer when Tasha said, "What did you expect? We're dealing with Helene Shaw here."

Sara tensed as the women stared at each other. Then, much to her confusion, Betty and Tasha cracked up laughing.

"You got me there, young lady. But next time, can you buy shorts, so we look like every other team in the league?"

Tasha leaned over the counter and patted Betty on the arm.

"I ordered them last night. The catcher called me complaining. I had no idea the ruffle would be a problem. I thought it was a cute look. Lesson learned."

Her sister's response surprised her. Whatever change had happened to her a few months ago seemed to be systemic. It wasn't that Tasha was just standing up against her ex-husband. She now had the confidence to assert herself everywhere. Timid and self-conscious Tasha was no more. In her place was a fearless woman.

"And what are you doing, lurking in the doorway, missy?"

Betty's question startled Sara, and she looked up to see two sets of eyes staring at her. Before she could answer, Tasha turned to Betty.

"You know, it was Sara's idea that I buy the uniforms. Why didn't you get on her case about the ruffles?"

Sara walked to the counter. Betty smiled at her as she said,

"Because she's my attorney, and I wouldn't put it past her to raise her hourly rates to cover the cost."

"Excellent point," said Tasha before she turned to her sister. "I didn't expect to see you today. How's it going?"

Nodding because she didn't want to admit the truth, Sara said, "I'm hungry. I thought I'd get lunch today."

Betty frowned.

"If you'd have called, I could've brought it to you," said Betty. "We have a meeting in an hour or so."

Kicking herself for forgetting, Sara struggled for an excuse. Since she didn't have one, she went with the truth. "I needed out of the office for a little while. Long morning."

She gave her order to Betty. The woman looked at her, started to ask a question, then shook her head and went to the kitchen. Grateful for the reprieve, Sara turned to her sister while she waited.

"I saw your email. Why'd you send it to me?"

Tasha shrugged. "You like to stay connected with the town news. I figured you already knew, but I wanted to be sure."

"You worried about what Doug might be up to?"

"Not in the slightest. It is the oddest feeling to not care anymore. Freeing, but still odd." Tasha cocked her head to the side. "It's not like you to take a break for lunch. Anything wrong?"

Standing up straighter, Sara thought, *trust Tasha to pick up on my mood.*

Unsure how much she should say, she relaxed when Tasha continued, "Do you want company? I could ask Betty to make me something. I came by to get a pie for the kids, but I've got time if you want to hang out. It's a nice day. We could eat in the park."

"I had the same idea," said Sara.

Her sister smiled back at her before she called out, "Betty, can you make me a lunch, too? Chicken salad sandwich?"

Betty's voice drifted out from the kitchen.

"Should I put them in the same bag or separate one?"

"Together," called back Tasha. "And can you hold my pie for me? I'll come back after Sara and I eat lunch."

The sisters stood in companionable silence while they waited for Betty. It didn't take long for the store owner to come out with a big bag in her hand. Handing it to Tasha, Betty motioned to the cash register.

"One mac and cheese and one chicken salad sandwich. I threw in some lemonades, too," she said.

The thought of so much food made Sara promise herself an extra yoga class over the weekend, but she didn't make a stink about it. Betty's food was the best in town.

Before she could get her wallet out, Tasha paid for the food, scooped up the bag, and headed out the door. Sara protested her sister's payment, but Tasha shrugged. "You can pick up the tab next time."

The two of them waved to Betty and headed out the door.

"Let's walk to the park. It'll only take a couple of minutes," said Tasha lifting the bag. "And I can tell you're already calculating how to burn off all the calories in here!"

Sara nodded and fell in step as Tasha ran down what was going on at her house: the school career fair was coming up and Brad had volunteered to present. Thankful her sister hadn't asked her to participate, she was surprised when Tasha said, "I hope you're not upset I didn't invite you. I figured you were busy."

"No, thanks. You're right. Too much going on right now." Sara decided she might as well tell Tasha what she'd found out from Ron. "We need to talk about that article you sent me."

Tasha kicked a rock off the sidewalk as she said, "I told you. It doesn't bother me that Doug's back in town."

They reached the park entrance and headed to a picnic

bench. Sara let her sister unpack the food before she continued the conversation.

"Ron Walters and I talked today."

Her statement had the desired effect. Tasha stopped what she was doing. "Why did you do that?"

"Curiosity. Something doesn't make sense about this project," said Sara. "The town needs it for sure, but why would Doug be the project lead? He hates this town and doesn't even live here anymore. Plus, his DUI getting dismissed is irregular to say the least."

"Can we eat while we talk?" Tasha looked up as she opened a container of coleslaw. "I'm on a schedule today."

Her sister's comment made her pause.

"Since when do you have a schedule?"

Tasha stuck her tongue out.

"If you want to talk, talk. But don't make fun of me."

Glad that her sister was able to take a joke, she continued, "Ron thinks The Miller Agency got Doug's DUI dismissed."

"Not my problem." Tasha took a bite of coleslaw and chewed it slowly before she continued, "I thought Doug wasn't paying his attorney anymore. Why would Ron talk to you about it?"

"Wow. I didn't think you paid attention to anything I told you."

Picking up her sandwich, Tasha said, "It's the new me," then took a bite. Globs of chicken salad fell out of the sandwich and landed onto Tasha's pants before it splatted to the ground. Sara noticed the ants start swarming when they realized lunch was served.

Sara handed her sister a napkin.

"The new you is still a messy eater. You might want to work on that around Greg."

Wiping off her pants, Tasha nodded. "True. But don't change the subject. Why are you telling me this? I don't care what Doug is doing. If he's got himself mixed up in some scheme, that's his problem. Not mine. And how did you know to call Ron? His name wasn't in the newspaper article I sent to you."

Pushing around the mac and cheese with her fork, Sara debated how best to tell her sister the bad news. Tasha must have sensed her hesitation because she said, "Go ahead and spit it out. This has something to do with me, doesn't it?"

Sara dropped her fork and nodded.

"Ron told me about Doug's plan." As Tasha stared back at her, Sara said, "Apparently Doug decided that now that he's back in town, you'll start paying all his bills again."

8

"Well, he can shove it where the sun don't shine. Why would he think I'd give him money?" Tasha asked, standing up. As she stood, she stepped into the chicken salad on the ground, mashing it everywhere. "Seriously? How did I manage this?"

Without answering, Sara helped her sister wipe off her shoe and clean up the mess. She wasn't sure how she expected Tasha to react, but this wasn't it.

"Are you sure this is what's going on?" Tasha asked as she pulled hand sanitizer out of her purse. Pouring some into her hands, she offered the bottle to Sara. Sara grabbed it and cleaned her hands while Tasha continued, "There isn't any way he can come after my money, is there?"

Shaking her head, Sara said, "As far as I know, no. The court approved everything. Doug doesn't have any right to what's yours. I was more concerned with how you'd react to him being back in town. And the answer is, you don't care."

"Not one iota. The kids might want to see him, but that might even be a stretch. Libby stopped asking long ago and after the car accident, Blake lost respect for his dad."

The sisters ate the rest of their lunch in silence. After cleaning up the trash, they headed back to Betty's.

"Mom called me this afternoon. She was irritated to learn Doug was back in town. Why didn't you tell her?" Sara asked.

As they walked into the parking lot, Tasha put her hand on Sara's arm.

"You should be glad she focused on Doug. I'm surprised she didn't offer to sign you up for speed dating."

Shaking her head, Sara knew her sister was right.

"I'm not speeding dating." She held up her hand before her sister could answer. "I heard more than enough about it from you. Don't you remember complaining about how the men had an unfair advantage?"

"But I met Greg there and I wouldn't be dating him if I hadn't let Mom badger me into it."

Sara pulled her keys out of her purse before she looked her sister in the eye.

"Greg is Blake's soccer coach. You already knew him. You didn't need speed dating for that. I've heard you say the only thing speed dating did for you was introduce you to all the crazy people out there."

"I'm also averse to sequins and leopard print now. Don't forget that," Tasha said. "But it also got me out of my comfort zone. Who knew I'd be able to walk into a room full of men and have an innocuous conversation?"

"I'm an attorney. I can interrogate anyone."

"That's not the point. The point is to find someone you're comfortable with," Tasha said. She pointed at the door to the coffee bar. "I have to run in and get the pie. You want to come to dinner Sunday?"

Sara gave her sister a hug.

"I'd love that. Text me the time and what I can bring. Tell Betty I'll see her at the office."

With that, Sara walked to her car and unlocked it. Her cell

phone rang as she turned the ignition. She waited for the phone to connect to her hands-free application before answering.

"Sara Shaw," she said, backing out of the parking spot.

A husky baritone she didn't recognize responded.

"Ms. Shaw, this is Jared Hughes at The Miller Agency. You spoke with my local counsel, Ron Walters this morning. I'd like to discuss your interest in our project."

Tapping the brakes, Sara put her car into park and stared at the speaker.

Thanks a lot, Ron, for running to your boss.

"I did contact Mr. Walters. I had a few questions about why you put Mr. Gerome in charge of the effort."

A chuckle met her ear and sent a shiver down her spine. Sara recognized her response. This man's voice interested her. A sinking feeling replaced the shiver.

Oh please. Now is not the time for another crush. If I had a therapist, they'd have a heyday with this.

"I wouldn't call Mr. Gerome the *head* of the project. More like... the *face*." Jared paused. "He's our spokesperson. For the moment."

"Why do you need someone local, Mr. Hughes? You seem capable of speaking as far as I can tell." She didn't want Jared to know she'd researched him and discovered he was the usual spokesperson for his projects, as well as a frequent witness in land development legal cases. Plus, he spoke at conferences and seminars on the same subject. The man was a well-respected expert. Doug's involvement still didn't make sense especially since he no longer lived here.

"As I'm sure you can guess, it's helpful to have local eyes on the ground. Mr. Gerome is a well-connected architect in town. He'll be guiding the process through the correct channels."

The lightbulb went on. Tasha's money was safe. Hughes' might not be, though.

"Mr. Hughes, as someone with *local eyes on the ground*, I have to tell you: you've got the wrong person on the job." Her tingles for the man disappeared when she realized he didn't know he had the wrong brother. "Regardless of what Ron told you, Doug Gerome isn't going to be an asset. He's a liability."

The throaty laugh was back again, this time irritatingly so.

"Mr. Gerome told me you'd say that. You're his ex-sister-in-law, if I'm not mistaken?"

"Yes, that's true," said Sara. "But did Mr. Gerome mention he has a brother? A brother who is an architect?"

Sara sat patiently as she listened to the silence. She watched as a woman walked her dog past the car while she waited to see how Jared was going to react. He cleared his throat before he continued.

"You're saying there are two Mr. Geromes?"

"Yes, there is Doug and there is his brother, Brad," said Sara. "Mr. Walters should've shared that information with you. You sure you got the right local counsel?"

"I'm beginning to wonder. Doug wouldn't happen to be an architect too, would he?"

"No, he's not. I'm surprised you couldn't tell."

Again, the line went silent and Sara waited. This man was used to being in control of the situation, but this time he'd been played. She had a hard time thinking Ron was behind this, but the man was Doug's attorney. Doug surrounded himself with a lot of questionable individuals.

"Damn it. He talked a good game, but I never could get him to be too specific about things. You're sure about this, right?"

"What do I have at stake here? I want to make sure Doug the Douche doesn't do something else to hurt my family." Sara bit her tongue when she realized what she had said.

How unprofessional. I need to get back on my game.

Instead of being chastised, she heard laughter.

"That name suits him," Jared said. "I wish I'd thought of it."

Glad he has a sense of humor.

Out of the corner of her eye, Sara saw Betty's car drive out of the parking lot. She glanced at her watch and realized she needed to get back to the office.

"Is there anything else you need? I'm late for an appointment."

"I'd like to set up a meeting with you. I may be in the market for a new counsel. My assistant will be in touch."

Before Sara could respond, Jared hung up. Irritation coursed through her veins as she started the car. She was tired of men telling her what to do, but Betty would be cross if she wasn't there on time for their meeting. Figuring out what to do about Jared would have to wait until after her appointment.

9

Jared stared at the phone on his desk. How did he get himself mixed up this in this crap? When he'd come to The Miller Agency, all he wanted to do was get away from the Hollywood craziness. Dealing with entitled celebrities was draining, not to mention damaging on his ethics. He learned fame didn't make a good person. Jared wasn't cut out to save his clients from their own poor choices, so he switched to property development. He hoped it was a way to stay in law but not deal with aggressive, unethical clients.

It was easier in a way. No clients to call him at all hours of the night, begging him to fix whatever situation they found themselves in. The Miller Agency offered an easy career option. What could be so difficult about fixing up properties and leasing them? Find an on-site project manager and let them handle all the details. It had worked in a dozen other cities. Why couldn't it work here?

He pushed back from his desk and stood up. Walking to the window of his corner office, he looked down on the city below. The Miller Agency conveniently neglected to tell him building renovations were as complicated as Hollywood. Passionate citizens fought for their towns, like celebrities fought for movie roles. Maybe he should've stuck with movie stars.

A discrete cough at the door caught his attention and he looked over.

"Excuse me, Mr. Hughes. I have some things that need your attention," his assistant, Monica, said. She waited by the door, holding a stack of paperwork. "Where would you like them?"

"On the desk, please," said Jared. Monica sauntered past him. He knew she'd taken this job to find a man. Everyone in HR knew about it. Another attorney warned him to keep his distance, but Jared didn't need warning. He had seen the consequences of mixing work and pleasure, and he had no interest in starting a bad habit now. Monica leaned over the desk, lower than necessary, and placed the stack of files front and center. Her already too short skirt rose up, giving him a peek of the lacy undergarment she wore underneath. He turned back to the window. No sense giving her the satisfaction that he was watching. "Hold my calls for the rest of the afternoon please."

He smelled Monica's thick perfume as she made her way back to his office door. His nose began to itch as the scent irritated it. Whatever floral concoction she was wearing must have lilacs in it. Jared hated lilacs.

"Let me know if you need anything else, Mr. Hughes. I'll be right outside."

With only a nod, Jared turned back to his desk to see what files she'd left. The door clicked shut and he let out his breath. Alone again, safely in his office, without the husband-hunter on the prowl. At least his celebrity clients weren't that obvious.

Making quick work of the files on his desk, Jared signed, dated, and completed the forms Monica had marked. The woman might be socially challenging, but she did know her job. Time spent on routine office work was at its lowest, thanks to Monica.

"If only she would husband hunt someplace else," he

mumbled. Jared grabbed the last file and flipped through it. "Damn it. This idiot again."

He skimmed the collection of transcribed voicemails, emails, texts and letters Monica intercepted from Michael Seaton at Davis Investments. The man badgered Jared constantly despite being told "no" countless times.

At first, Davis Investments seemed like any of the other investors The Miller Agency partnered with on projects. But after some due diligence and asking around, Jared decided to pass. The company's returns seemed too good and too consistent, and Seaton offered little to no details on how he made his money. The setup smelled like the Bernie Madoff fiasco, so Jared removed Michael and Davis Investments from his list of possible business associates.

Michael persisted though, which is why Jared stared down at a dozen requests for a meeting.

"Okay, this is me saying no again." Jared typed up another letter declining a meeting with Michael. He emailed the draft to Monica, asking her to proofread it, print it out and bring it to him to sign the next day.

Pleased he completed his task, he turned to his earlier issue. Ron Walters and figuring out what exactly was going on with the renovation.

Tilting his head to the left, Jared breathed a sigh of relief at the popping sound. For a few minutes, his neck pain eased. He wouldn't have given up playing sports, but there was a trade-off. A dull ache resided in his neck and back most days, but he knew he wouldn't have gotten his college paid for without his time on the football field.

It made him an interesting applicant for law school, too. Not everyone could balance athletics and school and still have time for community service and a social life. It helped that Jared absorbed information quickly and worked well under pressure. He breezed through the LSAT, and he'd had his choice of law schools. Finding a job out of law school had been easy, too. Several firms recruited him for his fame on the college football field and he didn't object.

Kneading the knot of tension in his neck with one hand, he punched in Ron's number with the other. He waited as the phone rang and rang. Just when he thought the call was going to voicemail, Ron picked up.

"Hey, Jared. Almost missed you. I'm heading out for the day."

Shaking his head, Jared grimaced as his neck pain intensified.

"Well, good thing you answered. We have an issue."

Sounds of rattling keys filled the line.

"Is it urgent? I have a client in jail and need to go sort things out for him. Can I call you back tonight or tomorrow?"

"I don't suppose that client is Doug Gerome."

The noise from the keys stopped, and Jared knew he had Ron's attention.

"Attorney-client privilege, but no. This has nothing to do with Doug. What's going on?"

Closing his eyes, Jared used his free hand to rub his temple.

"Why did you let me believe Doug was an architect?"

Ron cleared his throat. While Jared had only met the man once, he recognized the classic tell of someone stalling. Sara was right. Ron had intentionally lied.

"It was a misunderstanding. You asked me to get Doug onboard, which I did. I didn't catch that you wanted an architect until after I'd already got things squared away with Doug. That's when I realized you meant Brad. It was too late then. Doug signed your nondisclosure agreement and the contract."

"Which can easily be revoked. Doug misrepresented himself. As did you."

The panic in Ron's voice was evident when he said, "Did Sara put you up to this? She called me and wanted information about the project. I told her exactly what I just told you. I did as I was instructed. You asked for Doug Gerome and you got him."

Feeling the aggravation well up inside of him, Jared said, "I asked for Gerome the architect. Feel free to review your emails if you need to."

The keys jangled again.

"After Sara called, I did review them. The emails stated Doug Gerome. Had you mentioned it before, I would've known you'd got the wrong brother. But as it stands, you're the one who asked for the wrong person and got him. Now if you'll excuse me, I have a client who needs assistance."

"You hang up on me, you'll find yourself replaced."

Silence greeted his comment, but he could hear Ron's breathing on the other end of the line.

"What do you want?" asked Ron. "I did what you asked me to do. Doug has followed your requests. What does it matter at this point?"

"I suppose you could say it's a matter of principle which I question either of you have."

Ron laughed. "Coming from one of Hollywood's finest clean-up artists, I have a hard time believing you know what principles are."

Jared's temper flared. He hated it when people made assumptions. From experience though, he knew he needed to stomp down on this insubordination before it got out of control.

"As my employee, Mr. Walters, you need to remember the job you were engaged to complete. You are bound by certain—" Jared paused, searching for the correct word, "—standards. Standards detailed in your employment contract. Sharing your thoughts and opinions are not part of that requirement and put you in a precarious position when you don't have all the facts."

"The facts right now are this: you lied to me and you have

put this project in jeopardy by including a man who recently had a DUI. I don't know how you got him out of that mess—"

"You told me you wanted him on the job," Ron interrupted. "No matter what. I didn't think you would mind if I took something from your playbook. Which you didn't until Sara came into the picture. Doug's an ass but Sara is a b—"

"Don't say it," Jared said. He could feel the veins bulging in his forehead. He felt protective over her, and he didn't want to hear anyone call her names. Even if he didn't know her very well. "I never told you to do anything for Doug. You came up with that gem on your own. I'll be in touch."

Slamming down the phone, Jared took a deep breath to steady his nerves. The old Jared would've kicked over his chair and cleared the desk contents with one swipe of his arm. The new Jared reached high in the air for mountain pose, bent forward at the waist and dangled his arms. He couldn't touch his toes yet, but he would get there sooner or later.

But his visit to check on the project and to meet Sara would definitely be sooner.

"What the hell," he said to himself as he straightened up, grabbed the phone, and punched in Monica's extension. She picked up on the first ring. "I need travel scheduled. Get me to Glen Valley as soon as possible. Standard car, hotel, flight. Any questions?"

He knew his tone was terse, but Monica replied, "I'll arrange it," and hung up. Resigned, he sat down and reviewed his calendar, making a list of things to do. It would help him keep focused while he traveled to no man's land.

10

Sara fumbled with her keys as she unlocked the back door of the law firm and headed to her office. Dropping her purse and briefcase next to her desk, she rubbed her eyes as she walked into the break room to get her morning coffee. She usually grabbed some at home, but her Monday morning yoga class ran longer than expected. Since Renee always had coffee ready to go, Sara planned to make up time by grabbing her first cup at the office.

Only the break room light was off, and the coffee pot was empty.

"Damn it," said Sara to the empty room. "Renee's on vacation."

Her brain shifted gears as she thought through the receptionist's morning routine. She should have come by Sunday afternoon after the picnic at Tasha's to prep the coffee, but she forgot. Thankfully, the temp would be here any minute.

Leaving the coffee situation for the temp to deal with, Sara headed to her office. Despite being in a hurry, Sara followed her own routine. She booted her computer up, put her purse in its usual drawer, and stacked the contents of her briefcase neatly on her desk. Only then did she walk out to the lobby.

The room was dark, so she flipped on the lights and unlocked the front door. She returned to the receptionist's desk, turned on the computer and glanced around the desk to see what, if anything, Renee left for her. Luckily, a list of duties was laid out in the middle of the desk. Sara glanced through it and sighed in relief. Only a few easy projects needed to be completed. Nothing unusual or time consuming. Good. The temp should have an easy couple of days.

The chime on the front door chirped, and she relaxed even more. The temp had arrived on time. It might not be such a bad day after all. Looking up to greet her, the words froze in Sara's throat. The woman walking toward her was dressed like she was going on a date, not answering phones at a law firm. The woman's long brunette hair poufed out in all directions. A spaghetti-strap tank top boasting pink French poodles gave her the appearance of an overgrown toddler. Tight pleather pants completed the ensemble.

"You have *got* to be kidding me."

She realized her words weren't as quiet as she thought when the woman said, "Kidding you about what?"

Regaining her composure, Sara straightened up. There was no way this was the woman who would be sitting behind the desk all week. It had to be a walk-in client. Sara knew how to deal with those.

Sara plastered what she hoped was a smile on her face and said, "Welcome to Smith, Rogers & Shaw. How may I help you?"

The woman squinted down at the paper she held in her hand.

"The Orion Temp Agency sent me. I'm supposed to answer phones for a couple of days." She looked up at Sara. "Hey, you're Sara Shaw. Your sister is Tasha, right?"

Sara didn't know she could feel any more trepidation than she already did, but the woman's question made her nervous. There was something familiar about her, but she couldn't put her finger on it.

"Yes, I am," she said and extended her hand. "And you are?"

The woman shook Sara's hand, then dropped it before she said, "Brianna Thompson. You're prettier than I thought you would be."

Not sure how to respond, Sara ignored the comment and pointed at the papers on the desk. "Renee, our receptionist, wrote up everything for you. Why don't you read through it first, and then you can ask me any questions you might have?" The hope of coffee disappeared when she saw the look of confusion on Brianna's face. "Is there a problem?"

"It's just that I haven't had a cup of coffee yet, and I need some caffeine to jump start my brain," said Brianna. Why hadn't the agency sent over someone who knew to come to work prepared? Wait, she was craving coffee as well. Maybe she should get off her high horse and give this woman a break. "Do you have any coffee? I'd be happy to pick some up if you like."

Brianna's offer softened Sara's resolve. She couldn't be that bad if she was generous enough to make a coffee run offer.

"That would be great," Sara said. She turned back and opened a drawer under the desk. Entering a code into the small safe, Sara opened the door and took out $40 of petty cash. Then, she grabbed a sticky note from the desk and wrote out a list of coffee orders for herself, Rich, and Bill. Handing the note and the cash to Brianna, she said, "Here's our usual order. Add yours to it and grab some pastries too. A mix of raspberry cream cheese ones and chocolate will work. Half dozen is fine. We don't have many clients today. I wrote down the address of Betty's Coffee Bar. We're regulars there. Also, ask Betty for a fruit salad. Tell her it's for me. She'll know what to give you."

Brianna frowned.

"I don't believe in processed foods."

The statement caught Sara off guard. She debated arguing the point. If she did, it would slow down the caffeinating process, but she decided she had to know.

"How can you not believe in something that exists?"

A huge smile broke out on Brianna's face.

"Now that is a first. No one else has challenged me from that angle. You are good."

The comment made Sara pause. While she was good, why would the temp make that statement? Coupled with Brianna's remark about her appearance, it felt like Brianna had researched her before showing up to the job. Before she could follow up on the suspicion, the front door opened, and Bill walked in.

"Good morning." He nodded at Sara before seeing Brianna. She saw a flicker of surprise before his professional mask slipped into place, the one he used with clients. Putting down his briefcase, he held out his hand. "William Smith. Are you here for an appointment?"

Holding her own, Brianna's hand shot out as she introduced herself. "I'm Brianna Thompson. I'll be your temp receptionist for the week." Brianna looked over at Sara, who was still holding out the note and cash. To Sara's surprise, Brianna took it out of her hand and turned to the door. "I was leaving to get coffee and Danishes. Are you the raspberry or chocolate pastry?"

What the hell just happened? The woman doesn't believe in processed food.

"Raspberry. Did Sara give you my coffee order?" He glanced over at Sara. If she didn't know better, she thought he was holding back a smile.

"It's all on the list," Sara said pointing at the note in Brianna's hand. On impulse, Sara added, "Brianna was telling me she doesn't believe in processed foods."

A sense of unexpected guilt washed over her as she saw a flush of embarrassment color Brianna's cheeks. The guilt deepened when she noticed Bill's stern look of disappointment directed her way.

Nice job, Sara. Alienate the temp in the first five minutes and irritate Bill. Great way to start the day.

Brianna rallied first.

"Ms. Shaw misunderstood. I personally don't eat anything processed, but I would be happy to run to Betty's for you." Sara thought she detected irritation in the woman's voice but remained silent to see how the situation played out.

Bill looked back and forth between the two women. Sara recognized the expression and could almost read her partner's mind.

This one is going to give you a run for your money.

Picking up his briefcase, Bill started back to his office. "Well, if you have any questions, Betty knows what we like. She'll help you out. Sara, when you have a minute, can you come see me? I reviewed those documents over the weekend. There's a few things that need to be addressed." Without waiting for an answer, Bill walked out of the lobby.

Despite her irritation with Bill's comment, Sara focused back on Brianna. She noticed a change in the woman's demeanor and attempted to get things back on track.

"Betty's is only five minutes from here." Sara glanced at her watch. She planned to give the agency a call as soon as possible to confirm Brianna was really the person they'd sent. Something wasn't right, and she wanted to figure it out before Brianna got into the client files. "See you in a few minutes."

With a curt nod, Brianna left, and after the door clicked shut, Sara hurried to her office. A few minutes later, she sat looking at her desk. Brianna was in fact the right person. She was insured, bonded, and highly recommended, pink poodles notwithstanding. There was no reason Sara should be concerned. Before she could decide how she felt about the matter, Bill poked his head in the door.

"What the hell was that about? Why do I care if a temp believes in processed foods or not?"

Cringing at Bill's reaction, she explained.

"I asked her to pick up some pastries at Betty's. When she told me that she didn't believe in processed foods, I questioned her," she said, leaning back in her chair. She knew what she asked next was going to get a grouchy response as well, but she had to ask it. "Did you get a weird feeling from her? Like she knows more about you than she should?"

Bill's torso appeared in the doorway and he crossed his arms over his chest.

"Sara, what's going on with you? If I didn't know better, I'd suspect you were going soft on me. Since when do you believe in intuition for anything? I thought it was just the cold, hard facts for you."

She winced as she heard her own words repeated back to her. When she'd interviewed for the job, she emphasized her belief in following the law, regardless of the circumstances of the situation. Sara regretted her stance now. She blamed her black-and-white viewpoints on her immaturity and lack of experience. But Bill didn't let her forget what her younger self said.

Straightening up, she looked him in the eye.

"I believe in facts and research. But something about her seems off to me."

A grin crossed over Bill's face and he walked into the room. He took a seat in a side chair before he asked, "Really? And what did you do about it?"

"I called the agency, of course. They were able to confirm her identify and background." Sara fidgeted with the rake on her Zen garden, unaware that Bill's grin got bigger as she made lines in the sand. "But she seems to know more about me than a normal temp would. It feels like she's researched me. And Tasha." Dropping the rake, she looked up at Bill. She frowned when she saw the look on Bill's face. "What? Do you know what's going on?"

He slowly shook his head before he asked, "Did you ever meet Doug's girlfriend?"

Confused by the change in conversation, she shook her head.

"I didn't see the point."

"Well, if you had met China, you would notice that she looks a lot like Brianna."

Sara's heart sped up when she processed Bill's comment.

"That's not possible. There is no way the agency would send over China. Besides, her name is Brianna. Not China."

"Maybe Brianna is her real name."

An exasperated sigh escaped Sara's lips as she sank into her chair.

"You've got to be kidding me. How is it possible?"

"I think a better question is why is she here?" Bill said. "And do you need to tell Tasha?"

11

Sara looked at Bill.

"Knowing how much she hates this town, I'm surprised China'd tag along with Doug for a visit," said Sara. "But does Tasha really need to be warned about every little thing? Rich wanted me to call her about Doug and the riverfront building project and now you want me to call her about a temp you think might be China."

As she considered Bill's question, though, she realized he might be right. With Doug back in town, there were bound to be problems. During Doug's last visit, he asked his ex-wife several times for money and unsuccessfully blackmailed his brother, Brad, in addition to wrecking his rental car. He'd already told his attorney to forward his bills to Tasha. Who knows what else he was capable of?

And if Doug was in town, it made sense China would join him. Only, why would she give up a lucrative real estate career in Saint Thomas where they lived, to work as a receptionist in a town she despised?

Sara shook her head. Maybe she was overreacting. The entire thing might be innocent.

But Doug did lie to his new employer and Jared hinted he was in the market for another local counsel. Having Doug's girlfriend answering phones in Sara's office made it look like Sara supported both Doug and China.

Wait a minute! Who said Jared was asking me to be his local counsel? That is insane. He doesn't even know me.

A cough broke into her concentration, and Sara looked over to see Bill staring at her. Lost in her thoughts, she'd forgotten he was still sitting in her office.

"What? Don't you ever get sidetracked by something?"

"Sidetracked, yes. Pulled into the abyss, no," said Bill. "You planning to share what's going on or should I wait until you hire Doug, too?"

"Ha, ha. Like that would ever happen."

"So, tell me what you're thinking. China is going to be back soon."

Taking a deep breath, Sara relayed her thoughts about Doug and China. She reminded Bill about her conversation with Jared the prior week, how Doug and Ron lied to Jared so that Doug could be the face of the project. After she shared her thoughts, she smiled when Bill sat back in the chair with a look of confusion on his face.

"It's almost like we're watching a reality TV show, isn't it?" she asked. "I don't know what to think."

Bill frowned. "We should have Tasha come by. It may not be China after all. I could be wrong."

She shook her head.

"It isn't fair to make Tasha face the woman who ruined her marriage."

Bill stood up and walked back to the door.

"You and I both know the marriage was over. China was the final straw. Tasha is the easiest way to see what we're dealing with," said Bill. "You going to call, or should I?"

"Fine. I'll call her. But I want you and Rich around. Just in case."

Sara heard the lobby door jingle, signaling Brianna's return. She pointed at Bill.

"Get her settled, and I'll call Tasha."

Bill nodded and headed to the lobby. Sara ran her fingers through her hair in preparation for the crappy phone call she was going to have to make. She hadn't even had her coffee yet and she was going to have to ruin her sister's morning. Sara hated being the bad guy, but this morning, there didn't seem to be a choice.

Without further delay, Sara called her sister.

"Hello, the Gerome residence," Libby said.

Damn it. It's a school day. Libby shouldn't be home.

"Hey there, Libby, it's Aunt Sara. How are you today? And why aren't you in school?"

"We have the day off. It's a professional development day. Mommy's in the shower. Do you want me to leave her a message?"

"Yes, please. Tell her to give me a call as soon as possible. I have a quick question for her."

"Okay. Aunt Sara, are you going to come babysit us again? I liked it when you did."

A strange warmth spread in Sara's chest, and she smiled at Libby's words.

"I'd love to. I'll ask your mom about it when she calls me back."

"Good! Greg wants to take her away for the weekend and Mommy says no because there isn't anyone to watch Blake and me. Since you can, then she doesn't have an excuse anymore."

Sara's enthusiasm waned when she realized what she signed herself up for. Kicking herself for committing to something without all the details, she knew she didn't have a choice. Libby would be disappointed if she changed her mind.

"Okay. I'll talk to your mom," she said, trying to work up

some enthusiasm. "Love you. Talk to you later. Goodbye."

So that she didn't sit and stew about the call, Sara pushed away from her desk and headed to the lobby. Laughter reached her ears before she got to the others. As she entered the room, she noticed Bill and Rich on either side of the reception desk. Both held their coffee in one hand and a pastry in the other. Both laughed at whatever Brianna was saying.

"What did I miss?"

Brianna shrugged as she picked up a container and a cup of coffee and handed them to Sara.

"Here. Betty said you needed some variety, so she included a pastry for you too." Brianna slid a white bag toward Sara. "She also said to tell you 'don't shoot the messenger'."

The men stopped laughing when they saw the look on Sara's face.

Rich held out his coffee as he said, "She means well. Betty didn't want to upset you. And Brianna is the messenger, remember?"

Before she could answer, the phone rang. Panic shot through Sara. The call was most likely from her sister and Brianna/China was about to answer the phone. There wasn't anything she could do, so she held her breath when Brianna picked up.

The temp glanced down at the papers in front of her before saying, "Smith, Rogers & Shaw, LLC, how may I help you?" She nodded before saying, "One moment please." She tapped a button, replaced the receiver, and looked at Sara.

"Your sister is returning your call. Do you want to take it here or should I send it to your office?"

Seeing the curious look on Bill's face, Sara picked up her food and turned back to her office.

"I'll take it in private."

She walked as quickly as she could without looking as though she was running.

12

The blinking light on the phone told Sara what line Tasha was holding on. Setting down her food, she grabbed the phone and said, "Tasha, thanks for calling back."

"Is everything okay? Libby thought you sounded upset. She actually came into the bathroom and got me out of the shower," said Tasha. "I still have shampoo in my hair and it's cold standing here in a towel. What's going on?"

Despite the situation in the lobby, the image of her sister made her laugh.

"Paybacks are complete then. Do you remember when you set off the fire alarm in the house while I was in the shower?" The image of her teenage self still made her cringe. "I had to run outside in my towel and slippers with my hair dripping wet. Corey Hamilton saw me. You laughed about it for days. Be thankful no one is at your house to see."

"Oh my God! Are you telling me this call is retribution because the star basketball player saw you without make-up twenty years ago?"

"Absolutely not," said Sara, a grin still on her face. "It's a coincidence." The thought of China sitting in the lobby sobered Sara. "I need your help for something else though. Do you have time to come by the office today?"

"Do not chase your sister around, Blake! Someone is going to get hurt!" Sara pulled the phone away from her ear as she listened to Tasha chastise her son. "Sorry. I don't understand why the kids have so many days off school."

Sara switched the phone to her left ear. Her right ear was ringing from her sister's yelling.

"The kids can come too. I need you to take a look at something." She debated for a minute. If she told Tasha what she was up to, her sister might not come. On the other hand, it wasn't nice to force her sister to meet up with the woman who helped destroy her marriage. "I have to warn you though. It might not be pleasant."

A loud crash sounded followed by her niece and nephew screaming at each other.

"And you think this is pleasant?" Tasha asked. "What could be worse than seven-year-old twins fighting like cats and dogs?"

Closing her eyes, Sara knew she had a choice. She could spare her sister, or she could get the correct answer to the puzzle.

Tasha can handle it. She's strong enough.

"China is in town. At least, I think it's her. You're the only person I know who can confirm it though."

The kids' bickering was the only reason she knew Tasha was still on the phone. Sara heard Blake call Libby a name that was not appropriate for a seven-year-old, but Tasha didn't respond. When Libby followed up with a few choice words of her own, Sara asked her sister, "Do you need to call me back? Sounds like the kids need some intervention."

"Hold on a second." Before Sara could respond, Tasha called to the kids, "Both of you. To your rooms. Right now. When you can speak politely to each other, we'll discuss your consequences." A flurry of arguments filled Sara's ears, but silence soon followed. "Okay. Did you really ask me to identify China? That makes it sound like she's dead."

"No, she's alive and kicking. Renee is out of town—"

"She took some vacation?" Tasha interrupted. "Good for her!"

"Not good for me. We're busy over here. I got a temp and when she showed up this morning, something was off. Bill saw her and thought it was China."

"I'm guessing she gave you a different name or we wouldn't be having this conversation."

"Yes, she said her name is Brianna Thompson."

"That doesn't ring any bells, but I never asked if China was her real name. At the time, I wasn't interested in any of the details about my husband's mistress."

Sara cleared her throat and shifted in her seat, remembering how painful the divorce had been for her sister.

"Understood. But this woman is sitting at Renee's desk and I need to know if it really is China."

Sara wondered if the request sounded as lame to her sister as it did to her.

"Give me about thirty minutes and I'll be there," said Tasha, interrupting Sara's thoughts. "The kids have to come too. They can't stay here by themselves."

Feeling guilty about involving her niece and nephew, Sara said, "You don't have to bring them. I could come over and watch them while you're gone."

"Thanks for the offer, but these kids need out of the house. We'll come by, see you, then head over to Mom's for lunch. I will, however, take you up on the babysitting offer. Libby said you would babysit when Greg and I go out of town for a weekend. You sure you're up for that?"

The prospect of spending seventy-two hours babysitting didn't sound all that exciting, but she did owe her sister. Especially after what she wanted Tasha to do today. So, if watching the kids all weekend was what her sister needed, she would do it.

"Let me know the dates, and as long as I'm free, I'd be happy to help."

Tasha snorted. "Sara, you don't have a social life, so you will be free. I'll be there in a bit."

Glad to have a solution at hand, Sara hung up the phone and headed back out to the lobby. She found Brianna sitting behind the receptionist desk, staring down at some papers. Brianna looked startled when she approached the desk, but she smiled and asked, "What can I do for you?"

Not be China for starters, but who knows if I'll be that lucky?

She started to tell Brianna about Tasha's impending visit, but she hesitated. If Brianna was China, the news might scare her off. Instead, Sara asked, "Do you have any questions so far? Renee left some comprehensive notes so most of your responsibilities should be clear."

A bigger smile appeared on Brianna's face, one that appeared more genuine than before.

"These are the best instructions I've ever seen. My office should have something like this. It makes it so much easier when someone documents their responsibilities like this. You're lucky to have an employee like Renee. She's got things running like clockwork, doesn't she?"

Confused with Brianna's compliment, Sara asked, "Your office? You mean the temp agency?"

Brianna's smile dimmed as she waved her hand. "Oh. Yeah. That's what I meant. Anyway, you should definitely hang on to Renee. She's good."

"She is, isn't she." Sara didn't know what to make of China's comment. It left her feeling uncomfortable. Rather than stewing about it though, Sara said, "Since you seem to have this under control, I'm going to head back to my office. Feel free to call if you have any questions."

"I should be fine, but thanks." Brianna's gaze went back to the papers and Sara felt the uncomfortable sensation of dismissal. Rather than standing there, she walked back to her office and closed the door. Sara leaned back and closed her eyes. Why did she feel so uncomfortable around this woman?

"Damn it, Bill," she said to her empty office. If he hadn't put the idea in her head, she would be doing her morning work like she should be. Ready to get back to normal, Sara kicked off her shoes and stood in mountain pose to center herself. Once she was calm again, she sat down at her desk. "The woman is who she says she is and nothing else. Now focus on work, Sara, before you really get behind."

With that, Sara settled in at her desk and tried to work.

13

"Why are we visiting Aunt Sara at her office?" said Blake as he tossed his miniature soccer ball in the air. "Are we in trouble? Or did Daddy wreck his car again? That's the last time we got to visit Aunt Sara at work."

"Grandma said Daddy isn't supposed to drive anymore. And I know I'm not in trouble. I haven't done anything wrong," said Libby, swatting the soccer ball out of the air and catching it. "You got called into the office again, didn't you? Mommy hired Aunt Sara to defend you from the principal. What did you do this time?"

The bickering grew worse, but Tasha kept quiet. She'd hoped that as the kids got older, they would grow to be more respectful of each other. Her mother reminded her of how much she and Sara fought as kids, but that didn't help. She hated playing referee, and that was all she did lately.

As a single parent, she didn't get much of a break and it was taking its toll. Greg was a great help. Dating him made life more fun, but more complicated at the same time. They needed some time away to make sure their relationship was good for them, not just for the kids.

Blake and Libby adored Greg. Libby even asked if they would get married. She didn't want to pressure Greg, but she also worried that Greg wanted a family. He'd have an instant family if they got married, but he might want children of his own. Tasha didn't know if she was up for babies again.

The thump of the ball hitting her seat jolted her back to reality.

"Hey, I'm driving here. It's dangerous to distract the driver."

The kids laughed and Tasha glanced back at them in the rearview mirror.

"Mommy, you've been sitting in the driveway forever," said Libby. "Blake wanted your attention. We thought you left something inside."

Mumbling under her breath, Tasha put the car in gear and pulled into the street.

"You didn't answer Blake, Mommy," Libby continued. "Why are we going to Aunt Sara's office?"

Stopping at the intersection, Tasha waited for the trash truck to turn before she continued down the road.

"I have to identify something for Aunt Sara. She isn't sure if a person is who they say they are. Aunt Sara thinks I'll be able to tell."

She peeked in the mirror and saw the kids looking at each other.

"What's *that* look for?" Tasha asked. "I can help out my sister every once in a while."

The question caused the kids to start laughing, which confused Tasha even more.

"Now what is it? You two are up to something aren't you?"

More giggles followed and Tasha turned her attention back to the road. The kids could be stubborn, and she knew if she kept asking for answers, she would get none. If, on the other hand, she ignored them, they would be clamoring to tell her the scoop.

Two minutes later, her plan worked. Blake spilled the beans first, followed by Libby.

"We're going so Aunt Sara can babysit us," said Blake, throwing the ball into the air again. "It's a surprise so Greg can take you on a trip!"

Assuming Libby told her brother about Sara's offer to babysit, Tasha shook her head. "Not this time. I have to get the dates to Sara first."

While she wouldn't put it past Greg or her mother to arrange a secret trip, she knew that wasn't the case today. Sara sounded too stressed on the phone for this to be any kind of surprise. As the kids started arguing again, Tasha wondered how she would react if it turned out to be China sitting in the office.

She had a hard time believing it was really her, though. The woman hated Glen Valley and avoided it like the plague. Plus, China's job as a real estate agent tied her to Saint Thomas. China wouldn't give up a tropical paradise to live in what she referred to as the "most ass-backwards, Podunk town in the country". Or would she?

On the flip side, Tasha knew how persuasive Doug could be. He orchestrated their entire marriage, always manipulating things to get his way. For God's sake, it wasn't that long ago that she'd actually considered giving Doug a loan for a business investment. She gripped the steering wheel just thinking about it. But if he could manipulate his ex-wife, imagine what he could convince his current girlfriend to do.

Forcing her fingers to relax, Tasha took a deep breath. Until she got to the law office, there was no reason to get upset. She'd deal with China if she had to.

Pulling into the parking lot of the law firm, Tasha muttered under her breath, "Time to find out," before she called out to the kids, "Okay, we're here. Please use your indoor voices, no running and no fighting." She parked the minivan and turned to look at them. "One other thing: there might be other people in the office. Be nice to them."

Tasha felt guilty not preparing them for what they might find inside. She started to say something, but as she did, Blake threw the soccer ball at Libby's face. Her daughter's hands didn't come up in time to block it. After the ball connected with her nose, blood gushed down Libby's shirt.

"I'm sorry! I'm sorry!" cried out Blake. "I didn't mean to do that!"

"Yes, you did! You always do mean things." Libby's voice was muffled as she cupped her hands over her face. Tasha grabbed the roll of paper towels she kept in the car and tore off a handful. She turned back toward Libby and pushed the towels into her hands. "Ouch, Mommy! Don't touch my nose! It hurts."

Knowing this wasn't the first, nor would it be the last time this happened, Tasha hopped out of the minivan and ran to the passenger side to help her daughter out. She called back to Blake, "Grab my purse and lock the door, then come inside. We'll discuss your consequences later."

With a trail of blood behind them, Tasha led Libby to the office door. She heard the minivan beep when Blake locked it, so she slowed down to let him catch up with them.

"Open the door please and let Renee know that we need an ice pack and more paper towels."

"Mommy, I'm really sorry. I didn't mean to hit Libby," said Blake. Tasha thought he sounded like he was pleading with her. When she didn't respond, he started in with his sister. "Libby, it was an accident. It was."

"Blake. Get the door and talk to Renee. We will discuss this later."

This time Blake did as he was told. He propped open the door and called inside. It wasn't until she walked into the lobby of the office, she noticed anything was wrong. Blake stood silently in the front of Renee's desk. His mouth opened but no words coming out.

"What's the problem, Blake? Why don't you have the ice packs already? Or the paper towels?"

She'd never seen Blake's face so white. That was when she remembered why she was at the office. She didn't need to see who was sitting behind the desk to know what was bothering Blake.

"Honey, it's okay. Walk back to Aunt Sara's office. She'll be able to help."

Her son didn't move. He stared at the woman behind the desk for a long minute before he turned to his sister.

"Is that who I think it is?" Blake asked as he pointed.

Libby's eyes watered as she followed Blake's finger. It took her daughter a few seconds to understand what Blake was pointing at, but Tasha felt Libby tense up when she recognized the woman.

"Yup," said Libby, her voice muffled. "That's Daddy's girlfriend."

Without so much as a response, China picked up her purse and moved toward the door.

"Briana, wait a minute? Where are you going?" Sara asked as she walked into the lobby. The expression on Sara's face changed from curiosity to concern at the sight of Libby's blood. "Holy crap. What happened?"

Before Tasha could explain, China inched closer to the door, but Blake positioned himself between his father's girlfriend and her escape route. Tasha recalled seeing his father do exactly the same thing when he didn't want someone to leave.

Maybe Doug taught the kids something useful after all.

Realizing she was trapped, China turned to Tasha.

"It's so good to see you and the kids. Blake, you're quite the young man these days. And Libby." Tasha suppressed a laugh at the effort China made to come up with something positive to say about her daughter, whose face was a mess of paper towels and blood. "Well, you've grown up as well."

Libby groaned, reminding Tasha of her priority.

"It's okay, Libs. We'll get you fixed up." Out of the corner of her eye, Tasha saw China inch closer to the door. "Sara, your temp seems to be leaving. Can you keep her for a minute while I help Libby? I'd like to have a word with her."

"Bill and I can handle it," said Rich as he walked into the lobby. "I have a few questions for Brianna as well."

"Who's Brianna?" asked Blake.

Sara glanced at Tasha and she nodded.

"That's Brianna, Blake," said Sara as she pointed. "She's our receptionist while Renee is out."

Blake crossed his arms over his chest and frowned.

"She's lying. That's China. Libby?"

Despite her condition, Libby repeated, "Yes, that's Daddy's girlfriend."

"Ex-girlfriend. It's over." China put her purse down on the desk and sat back down in the chair. "What a mess of a relationship."

"Excuse me," said Rich. "You don't need to share everything in front of the children."

Libby blotted her nose with the paper towel before she said, "It's okay, Mr. Rogers. Grandma told us all about China."

Blake nodded in agreement with his sister. "Yep. Grandma prepared us for whatever the homewrecker could throw at us."

Tasha bit the inside of her mouth to keep from laughing. She'd have to tell her mother to stop talking in front of the kids like that, but the expression on China's face was worth it.

14

Sara sat behind her desk, watching Blake play a game on his handheld device. Tasha dabbed at the dried blood on Libby's clothes.

"What did the agency say when you called them about Brianna/China?" Tasha asked. "Anything you can do about it?"

Sara shook her head.

"Brianna is her real name. Other than neglect to tell them she has a nickname, technically, she didn't do anything wrong. The assignment was done last minute, so it appears to be luck of the draw."

Throwing a used paper towel in the trash, Tasha frowned.

"It doesn't explain why she's in town. The woman hates it here. You heard that she and Doug aren't dating so why is she someplace she doesn't want to be?"

"No idea. I wonder if Mom knows?" asked Sara. Since Tasha arrived in the office, Sara had been waiting for Helene to call or show up. She didn't know why but her mother always seemed to know when something was going wrong. "Should we tell her?"

"Grandma already knows," said Libby. "She told me that she's all-knowing and it's no use to hide anything from her."

Sara looked at her sister for a second before they both busted out in laughter. They were still laughing when Bill poked his head in the door.

"You've found the humor in the situation, I see. Does that mean you know what you want to do about Brianna then? The woman has been sitting on the couch waiting while Rich is answering the phones." Bill sighed. "Renee makes it look easy. Rich keeps disconnecting people when he sends them to voicemail."

"I can help him." Blake looked up from his video game. "Ms. Renee showed me how one day when I was here." He stood up and looked at his mom. "Can I? Please?"

Tasha nodded and said, "It's okay with me. You have to ask Aunt Sara though."

Sara nodded as did Bill. Bill waved Blake over to him.

"Come on buddy. Let's go rescue Mr. Rogers!"

Blake hopped up, tossing his game device onto the couch.

"Can I get paid for this? I need some money for a new game."

"Blake! You're helping out, not bribing people," said Tasha as she grabbed another paper towel. "Be good."

The lawyer and Blake walked out of Sara's office.

"Mommy, can I go too?" Libby asked.

Sara saw the look on Tasha's face as she pointed at her daughter's shirt.

"Honey, I don't think you're in any condition to greet clients. Your shirt is all bloody."

Standing up, Sara walked to the door of her office and closed it. On the back were several dry cleaner bags. She flipped through a couple before pulling one off the hook and turning back to Libby. She held the melon-colored blouse out to her niece and said, "You could wear this. It will cover what you have on. Plus, the color looks good on you."

Sara's heart swelled when she saw the look of excitement in her niece's eyes.

"Mommy, can I? Please?" said Libby. She raced over to the shirt and held it in her hand. "It is so pretty! I love this color!"

Sara knew from the look on her sister's face that she would get a talking to for offering the shirt before asking, but it was worth it. Libby was definitely a "clothes" girl and Tasha was not. Even when they were kids, Tasha had no interest in wearing fancy clothes, shoes, or make-up. But Sara saw a lot of herself in Libby, and this was one way of fostering it.

"Calm down, Libby. You don't want to bleed on Aunt Sara's shirt," said Tasha. "Knowing your aunt, that blouse costs more than everything in my closet."

Grinning at her victory, Sara playfully argued. "You're the one who won the lottery. Why doesn't your closet have better stuff in it?"

"Really? You're asking that question, even though you've known me since birth and I've never, ever, in the entirety of my existence cared for shopping," said Tasha. "This is the same discussion we had when we shared a bedroom. I know you remember that."

The image of their childhood bedroom popped into Sara's head. Her side was pristine. Everything was in its place. The bed was made with hospital corners and she even had a vase of daisies sitting on her desk at all times. Tasha's side of the room looked like a tornado hit it. Clothes covered every surface and Sara didn't think the sheets on Tasha's bed had ever been washed. Dirty plates and glasses littered the desk, and the trash can overflowed with rubbish.

"Yes. I remember. How on God's green earth could I forget? You were the—" Sara stopped herself when she noticed Libby staring at her. "You were the best sister a girl could have."

Libby smiled and looked at her aunt.

"Can I go put this on?"

She nodded and watched as Tasha helped Libby button the blouse over her bloodstained shirt. The blouse resembled a dress, but it didn't bother Libby.

Her niece started out of the room but stopped abruptly. She rushed back to Sara and threw her arms around her waist.

"Thank you, Aunt Sara! This is awesome."

Without waiting for a response, Libby released Sara and darted out of the room.

Tasha watched her daughter leave before turning back to Sara.

"Thanks for not completely ruining my credibility."

Sara leaned her head back and closed her eyes.

"You were the dirtiest, most disgusting roommate in the entire world," said Sara with a smile. "But you're right. Libby doesn't need to know that."

"So, what are you going to do now? With China, that is?" Sara frowned when she heard the note of concern in her sister's voice. "You can't let her work here, can you?"

Walking over to the window, Sara said, "She's licensed, bonded, and insured. There is no logical reason I shouldn't let her work here."

Tasha raised her hand, as if she were an elementary school student.

"She slept with my husband. And if that isn't bad enough, she left your niece and nephew in a broken home." Tasha put her hands on her hips and frowned. "Although, she did admit to the relationship being over. I wonder what happened?"

Before Sara could speculate, her phone rang. She glanced at the extension and saw that it was reception.

"Hold on. Blake is calling me already." Sara ignored her sister's look of disapproval and grabbed the phone. "What's up, Blake?"

"Aunt Sara, this is awesome. As soon as I sat down, some guy came in the door asking for you. I got him coffee and everything."

Confused, Sara glanced at her calendar.

"I don't have anything on the schedule. Who is it?"

"Don't know," Blake said. Sara heard muffled voices, then the shuffle of the phone being handed over to someone else.

Instead of Blake's voice, Sara heard Bill whisper, "What the hell is Jared Hughes doing here to see you?"

15

Tasha watched her sister's eyes grow large. From the shocked expression on Sara's face, Tasha knew whatever Blake told her was unexpected. She frowned. It wasn't often that her sister got taken by surprise.

"He didn't mention he was coming. Damn it, he must have booked a flight right after we talked last week." Sara listened to the response on the other end of the phone while Tasha debated if she should just walk out to the lobby to see what was going on. Deciding that was the best idea, she stood up, but Sara waved at her to sit back down.

Reluctantly, Tasha dropped back in the chair and waited for Sara to finish the call. It didn't take long before her sister dropped the phone in the cradle. Instead of speaking, she stood up, kicked off her shoes, and did some sort of yoga pose.

"What's the problem?" she asked as she watched Sara move from one position to another. She knew it was some sort of flow sequence her sister used to de-stress. Tasha also knew it would be a few minutes before Sara would respond. Once her sister got started on her yoga-smoga crap, nothing got through.

Sure enough, three minutes later, Sara stood back upright and put on her shoes.

"I know what you're thinking, but you should try it sometime," said Sara. "Yoga calms you down."

Tasha shrugged.

"I am calm. It's you I'm worried about," said Tasha. "Who got on a plane after you talked to him? Better question: is Blake being good?"

Sara paced in front of the window as she answered, "Jared Hughes is in the lobby."

She waited to see what else Sara would say, but all her sister did was walk back and forth as if the path in front of the window had the answer she needed. Tasha scrunched her nose as she recalled where she knew the name.

"You mean the guy you were talking about on Sunday? The one that plays football?"

Sara nodded. "That's the one. He also happens to be in charge of the building renovation and is Doug's boss."

"Oh yeah. Now I remember." Tasha realized her sister was still pacing. Clearly, the yoga didn't calm Sara down. "Why is he in your office?"

"I don't know. He wanted to set up a meeting," Sara threw up her hands in frustration, "but I thought he would at least call before he showed up."

Tasha nodded despite the fact her sister wasn't paying attention. "Maybe he's used to people bowing down to him. Didn't you say he's a bigwig? People cater to bigwigs."

Sara continued as if she hadn't heard her. "But don't you think it is more than a coincidence that China and Jared show up on the same day, in my office, nowhere near where they are supposed to be?"

"China is here because you hired her. Jared is here because he said he wanted a meeting with you." Tasha kept her explanation simple, like when she explained math problems to

Blake. Too much detail and it sent her son over the edge. Sort of the way Sara looked right now. "Might you be overreacting?"

Sara's cheeks flushed when she said, "He gave me the tingles. When I talked to him on the phone, his voice just—I don't know. Sounded attractive."

Tasha let out a yelp.

"Well, you didn't tell me that."

Leaning over her desk, Sara said, "I'm a professional. Voices should not make me act like a teenager. What do I do?"

While matchmaking was more of Helene's thing, Tasha gladly advised her sister.

"Duh. Go out and meet the man. That's the only way you're going to know if it's anything more than you reacting to his smooth, sultry voice over the phone."

Tasha ducked as Sara threw a pen at her, but when she sat up, Tasha saw her humor had the desired effect. Sara looked calm again. Taking advantage of the moment, Tasha stood up and headed to the door.

"Wait for me," said Sara. "I should go out, too. Bill sent Jared to the conference room. I guess China was trying to hit on him."

Tasha laughed. "The woman isn't subtle. That's for sure. I'll take the kids home now that you know it's China."

She expected Sara to agree, until her sister asked, "Will you please stay? The kids can work the phones if you can go out and sit with them?"

Tasha didn't mind helping out her sister, but she had limits. "What about China? I don't want to spend any more time with her than I have to."

"I'll tell her we don't need her after all," Sara said as she gathered up a notebook and pen. As soon as she picked them up, she dropped them back on the desk. "Damn it. I hate being nervous."

Tasha wanted to laugh at her sister, but from the way Sara

was acting she knew that would be a bad idea. She couldn't resist teasing her though.

"Boys'll do that to you!"

Grabbing her notepad and pen again, Sara headed to the door. "I don't have time to listen to you make fun of me. I have to go see what Jared wants." As she reached for the door, she looked back. "Thanks for coming today. I know it wasn't easy."

Feeling pleased she could help her sister, Tasha gave her a quick hug and followed her out the door. She came to a stop when she bumped into Bill who was coming down the hallway.

"Sara, Brianna has to go. She's hitting on Jared and propositioned Rich while he was on the phone with the county judge. Judge thought it was funny once Rich explained who it was and what was going on, but we need to get things back in check."

Tasha grimaced at the thought of her children listening to China's shenanigans. "Are Blake and Libby still out there?"

"I sent them to my office since Brianna was acting so erratic. They don't need to be exposed to that kind of crap." He turned his attention back to Sara. "So, what do we need to do?"

Before Sara could answer, Tasha jumped in.

"Sara's going to the conference room to deal with the guy who just flew in. You and Rich can tell China she is no longer needed. As soon as you do that, the kids and I will man the phones," said Tasha. She crossed her arms over her chest. "But I'm not going back in there until that woman is gone."

Tasha saw Bill's eyes flick to Sara, who simply nodded.

"You heard the woman, Bill," said Sara as she strutted out the door. "Let's get this firm back in order."

16

Before Bill could argue, Sara headed to the conference room. She didn't know how her sister managed to pull her out of her funk, but Tasha was on a roll. There was no telling what she was capable of.

Sara stopped outside the conference room door and took a deep breath. She hadn't expected to meet Jared so soon, and she didn't know what caused the man to show up unannounced. She needed to be prepared for anything, especially since Jared thought he'd been played by Doug.

She quietly pushed open the door. The man standing at the window didn't turn around immediately, so Sara took a moment to assess her opponent.

That's not fair, she thought. *Maybe he will be on my side.*

Sara judged him to be at least 6 foot 5 inches, maybe taller. His sandy blonde hair looked ruffled, like someone had just run their hands through it. Her gaze lowered and admired the well-fitting athletic cut dress shirt that tucked into the black Armani dress pants. She grinned when she saw the dust on his Italian leather shoes. Clearly, he didn't know where he was going when he left the big city.

"Hello. Should I assume you're Ms. Shaw?"

The smooth tenor of his voice startled her. Being caught staring at him wasn't the way to make a good first impression.

She looked up at his face and was taken aback by the brilliant blue eyes that met her gaze. Sara froze under the intensity. Never before had she seen eyes that drew her in like that.

"Ms. Shaw?"

Realizing she'd been staring at him with her mouth open, she straightened as she put her notepad and pen on the table. She stepped toward him and extended her hand.

"Yes, this is quite the surprise, Mr. Hughes. I didn't expect to see you here this soon."

He took her hand and she was surprised again when the rough texture of his palm collided with hers.

He doesn't always sit behind a desk. What does he do in his spare time?

A few inappropriate images popped into her head and she could feel her cheeks get hot. Breaking the handshake as fast as she could, she waved toward the table.

"Please. Have a seat," she said. Seeing the pastries on the counter, she asked, "Can I get you coffee or something to snack on?" As the words came out of her mouth, she cringed. She sounded like a waitress, not an attorney.

What is going on with me? Get a grip on yourself.

Thankfully, he shook his head.

"I'm fine," Jared said as he pulled out a chair. Sara looked at him questioningly when he didn't sit down. Her cheeks reddened even more when he pointed at the chair and said, "After you."

Not sure why she hadn't realized what he was doing, she slid into the chair. Jared nodded then walked around the table and took his own seat. She sat there in awe of the situation.

"I don't have a lot of time in town, so if it's okay with you, I'd like to get down to business."

Startled into action by his words, Sara nodded.

"That's fine. When we talked, you mentioned scheduling an appointment to meet with me. I didn't realize you would be coming to town so soon."

Or without notice, she thought but kept that to herself.

Jared had the decency to look apologetic.

"This trip came about more suddenly than I expected. I should've given you a call instead of dropping in." He spread his hands out on the table in front of him. "It appears Ron Walters needs to be replaced."

Before she could ask what Ron did, the door flew open and Blake ran in. He ran around the table, oblivious to the two people staring at him. Without a word, he circled the table and left the room, slamming the door behind him.

Jared's lips curved up slightly and Sara's heart hitched. While she was glad he saw the humor in Blake's actions, she wasn't in the mood to explain why her nephew was here.

"Cute kid. Are all your clients so young?"

She relaxed when she took in his casual tone.

"Every once in a while," she said. Wanting to be truthful with Jared, she added, "Actually, that was my nephew, Blake. My sister came to the office to do me a favor and she brought the kids."

"He was the one who identified China."

The surprise of Jared knowing China's name made Sara forget what she'd planned to say next. She stared at the man as he continued without her feedback.

"Blake and Libby are friendly kids. They were more than happy to tell me who they were and why they were here." Jared leaned back in his chair and put his hands behind his head. At first, she thought he was being conceited, acting as if he were better than her. But something about his face changed her mind. He looked almost wistful.

"What I didn't understand was why your sister's ex-husband's ex-girlfriend is working as a temporary receptionist in your office?" The smile on his face was more visible now. "Blake couldn't quite explain that." She must have frowned at him because he sat forward, resting his elbows on the table. His smile dimmed. "Hey, don't get mad at the kids. I'm good at interrogating and getting information. They didn't have a chance against me."

"I read as much," Sara said. Jared's eyebrows furrowed, and she could only hope it was because it bothered him that she knew about his past. "Why did you leave Hollywood? You were good at it. Dealing with Doug can't be as satisfying."

"You'd be surprised. Movie star problems aren't that much different from your average Joe issues, except the celebrities aren't used to someone telling them no." He stood up and walked to the coffee set up. "I think I'll have some coffee after all. Would you like some?"

She shook her head. Jared turned to the coffee pot and Sara found herself staring at him again. Truth be told, she watched his butt, which looked toned and defined under the designer pants.

Pull your mind out of the gutter, woman. This is business. You need to focus.

Corralling her thoughts, she watched Jared as he took a sip of his coffee. His eyebrows went up and he nodded his appreciation.

"Not sure who is in charge of the coffee purchasing, but this is good stuff."

Rather than let him know that was her job, Sara looked back down at her paper. This meeting needed to get moving soon, or she was going to do or say something to embarrass herself, at least more than she already had.

"You were saying you need local counsel?"

She could tell the redirection of topic didn't go unnoticed, but Jared didn't say anything until he returned to his seat.

"Yes, and a new local figurehead. Doug isn't going to work out. The man isn't what he was billed to be." Jared put his mug down and propped his head on his clasped hands. "I have some ideas on replacements, but I'd like your input."

"You just met me. My input may not be any good," said Sara. "In fact, it might be worse than Ron's or Doug's. Why me?"

The sly smile crossed his face again as he spoke. "I did some research on you as well, Ms. Shaw. Your input is always good. At least, that's what everyone says."

Sara tamped down her excitement. Interesting that he'd researched her. While she was glad her hard work paid off, Sara was suspicious of people who buttered her up with compliments. Doubt replaced the excitement. Was Jared like everyone else in her life? Throw out a compliment then ask for help?

Her uncertainty must have showed on her face because he frowned. "What's wrong? You look like someone just stole your cookies?"

His attempt at a joke made her laugh.

"If I were Blake, that would make sense, but I'm an adult. You can't break the tension that fast."

"I just did," he said and pushed back the chair and stood up. At first, she thought he was going to move toward her, but instead he stepped to the other side of the table, crossed his arms, and leaned causally against the wall. "Sara Shaw, I don't think you're quite the hard-ass everyone says you are."

Part of her was thrilled that he considered her tough. Being a female attorney was difficult. She had a fine line to walk. Too much attitude and she was a bitch. Too little and she was a pushover. Hard-ass seemed like a good middle point for her.

The other part of her, however, was disappointed, but she didn't know why. She'd never met this man before, only talked to him on the phone once. She had no reason to care what he thought of her, personally or professionally. And yet she found herself leaning forward to hear what else this man would say.

"I need someone who can keep this project on track. My current local counsel lied to me and the head of the project isn't who I thought he was. You're local. You know this place. How about it?"

For the first time since he mentioned the position, Sara realized how much she wanted it. Something new and exciting to break up the monotony of the familiar and comfortable.

"Why me?" she asked. "I'm not the only attorney in town. I'm not even the only attorney in this office."

Jared's eyes narrowed and his mouth twitched. She considered it might be some sort of tell, but before she could decide where to steer the conversation, the phone rang.

Irritation surged through her, and Sara thought she saw the same in Jared.

"Excuse me. I need to get that."

Standing up, she turned her back to him to walk to the phone. If she didn't know better, she would've guessed his eyes were burning holes in her back. Jared Hughes wasn't used to being told to wait.

Well, tough cookies, thought Sara. *He could stand to learn some patience.*

Uncertain who would be on the other end of the phone, Sara said, "Hello? What can I help you with?"

"We have a problem," said Bill. "I need you out here. Actually, I think Hughes needs to get out here, too."

"Why do you need Jared's help?" asked Sara, her eyes flicking back to the man in question. When he heard his name, he frowned.

"What's going on?" Jared asked.

Sara motioned for Jared to wait as she listened to Bill.

"Doug Gerome and Ron Walters just showed up which sent

China into a tizzy, and Tasha's with the kids in my office. I need back up. Now."

17

Sara dropped the phone and headed to the door when Jared's voice stopped her.

"What's going on?"

She turned toward the man who inadvertently created more chaos in her life. The tone of his voice and expression on his face told her he expected an explanation. Maybe he would have a better way of solving this. Facing Ron and Doug wasn't something she looked forward to.

"Your former local counsel and head of the project are standing in the lobby. Not sure why but I suspect it has something to do with you," Sara said. She considered refraining from asking the next question but decided what the hell. "Does trouble always follow you to town?"

Sara walked to the door and threw it open without waiting for his response. Raised voices greeted her, and she took off in a sprint toward the lobby. Coming around the corner, she slid to a halt when she saw Tasha standing between China and Doug. Her sister resembled a referee. Tasha's arms extended, keeping the ex-lovers from coming into contact. Bill and Rich stood off to the side, each one behind a child. Blake and Libby cheered on their mom, which Sara realized was most of the noise she heard.

"You came back here for her, didn't you?" asked China.

Everyone's attention turned to Doug, who shrugged.

China screamed again.

"What makes you think she's better than me, anyway?"

"For one, she doesn't yell as much as you," said Doug with a grin on his face. "She also wouldn't beat me up like you're trying to do."

Tasha struggled to keep China from getting closer to Doug. "You know, I'm standing right here. I can hear everything you're saying about me. And please note, the kids are here too."

Throwing her arms up in the air, China said, "Yes, the same kids who positively ID'd me because your sister couldn't. Don't blame whatever happens on me. You didn't have to get involved in this."

Irritation flooded Sara, but before she could say anything, Jared walked by her and inserted himself into the situation.

"Back off. Everyone. Right now. Take a seat and we'll discuss this rationally."

"Look, man, this is none of your business," said Doug. He stood up straight, as if he could intimidate Jared. "Stay out of it."

Sara saw anger flash in Jared's eyes. As quickly as it flared, Jared contained it. His Adam's apple bobbed, and his fists clenched and relaxed.

Holy crap. He's going to take out Doug, thought Sara.

Jared stepped closer to Doug and stopped a few inches away.

"You are my business. I am your boss, at least for now. Leave these women alone."

A confused Doug looked over at Ron, who nodded. Without hesitation, Doug stepped away from China and Tasha. He walked to his attorney and asked, "This is Jared Hughes?"

Ron nodded again. "I tried to tell you earlier he was in town. Don't blame me if he fires you."

Before anyone could react, Tasha walked to the kids and took their hands.

"He's my ex-husband," she said to Jared, nodding her head toward Doug. "Anyone who fires him is a friend of mine. Now, if you'll excuse me, the kids and I are leaving."

"But, Mommy, we're going to miss all the excitement!" Blake stomped his feet on the floor as his mother pulled him toward the door.

"Don't worry," Libby told her brother. "Grandma will get the surveillance footage from the office so we can watch it."

Sara smiled when she heard Tasha say on the way out, "Under no circumstances are you to watch anything your grandmother shows you from this office. It is not appropriate!"

As the door closed behind Tasha, Doug rolled his eyes and said to Sara, "I can't believe Helene's still involved in every bit of her life. Why doesn't she grow up already?"

Sara almost missed China's left hook as it connected with Doug's face. While everyone was paying attention to Doug, China took advantage of the lull and attacked. As soon as the punch landed, she pounced on Doug, pushing him to the floor. He landed with a thud, and China continued with repeated blows to his torso, arms, and head.

Sara knew this type of behavior went on, but she'd never seen it firsthand. She waded into the fray, grabbing China by the hair and pulling her away. Sara expected Doug to follow, but somehow Jared hauled him off the floor. Keeping him off balance, Jared maneuvered Doug to one corner of the office and Sara pulled China to the other.

As Sara shifted to avoid China's other fist, she heard Rich say, "Unbelievable."

She shook her head when she heard Bill tell Rich, "We could mail a tape of this to one of those TV shows. The ones where the audience votes on who has the funniest home video? I think we'd have a shot at winning."

China struggled against Sara's hold on her hair.

"Let me go. You're hurting me," cried China.

"You hurt me, you bitch," said Doug from across the room. He rubbed his chin as he watched. "Sara, pull her hair harder. She deserves it."

"Enough," Sara yelled. Her raised voice shocked the entire room into silence. Even China stopped struggling. Embarrassed by her sudden outburst, Sara dropped China's hair and rubbed her hands down her legs, smoothing the wrinkles in her dress slacks. "We are all adults here. Let's act like it."

"Ms. Shaw is right," said Jared. "This was not how I intended to find my local counsel and project lead. You are both fired."

"I didn't do anything except my job." Doug pointed at China, rubbing his chin. "She showed up to make trouble. Things were fine until then." He turned back to Sara and smiled. "You impressed me, though. You wanna get coffee sometime?"

18

Jared balled his fist as he thought, *The audacity of this jerk.* What he wouldn't give to punch Doug in the face. Since he couldn't, he took a few quick yoga breaths and willed himself to calm down before anyone else noticed. His anger subsided to irritation as his fist uncurled and the furrows in his forehead relaxed.

"I think it's time you left." Jared glanced at Sara and she nodded her agreement. Her flushed cheeks made him wonder why she was embarrassed about Doug's come-on. For some reason, he didn't think she embarrassed easily, but he'd have to table that thought for later.

"You can't tell me what to do." Doug scowled and continued whining. "This isn't even your office."

"It is **my** office, and you should leave," Sara said.

Doug took a step toward Sara. Before Jared knew what he was doing, he positioned himself in front of her, his hands on his hips, blocking Doug's path.

"You heard her. Leave."

Taking a step back, Doug pointed a finger at Jared.

"You can't fire me, you know. We signed a contract," said

Doug. He tipped his head, as if he were attempting to look down his nose at Jared. "Besides, I'm the perfect person for this job. People know me here. My kids are here. I have ties to this community."

Before Jared could speak, China said, "I bet you haven't bothered to check on your kids once since you got here. You always told me you can't stand to be around them."

Jared watched Doug's face redden as he shifted his attention toward the other woman. He kept his eyes on Doug as he heard Sara speak up.

"Ron, you and Doug need to leave. Neither of you are welcome here."

Doug stomped his foot on the floor. The action reminded him of the temper tantrum the little boy had just before he left. "You can't tell me what to do. I don't care whose office we're in, but I'm not going anywhere until I know what's going on."

Doug shrank back when Jared spoke.

"I'll explain it. You had Ron lie to me to get a job you are not qualified for. You broke every clause in your contract. The behavior you exhibited in front of your children today was appalling," Jared glared at Ron as he continued, "and yours wasn't much better. I don't want to hear from either of you again."

"Come on, Doug. Let's get out of here." Ron took hold of Doug's arm, but Doug shrugged him off.

"You can't fire me. I have a contract."

Jared smiled.

"I wrote the contract, ergo, I know the termination clause in the contract. So yes. I can fire you."

For a few seconds, Jared wasn't sure what Doug planned to do. The sleazebag looked at Ron, who shook his head, then over at Rich and Bill, who both stood there looking amused with the situation. Doug's gaze skipped over China then settled on Sara, who stared back. Jared saw Doug swallow before he returned his gaze.

"This isn't over, Hughes! I'm not going to roll over and let you take this job from me." Doug's words lingered in the lobby as he followed Ron to the door. As the door slammed shut, Doug shouted "I'll be back!"

The words echoed in the lobby for a few seconds and then faded. Bill broke the silence when he said, "That sounded better coming from the Terminator."

Rich and China laughed, but Jared noticed they both stopped when no one else joined in.

"Your services are no longer needed, China. Or Brianna. Whichever it is," said Sara. "I'd suggest not coming back here again. Between lying to the agency and fighting with Doug, you've opened yourself up to all kinds of issues."

The woman picked up her purse.

"Fine. I don't want any trouble. I only came to town to get the money that Doug owes me," she said as she smoothed down her pink tank top. "And I never lied about who I was to the temp agency. My real name is Brianna, and I have excellent references."

Curiosity got the best of him and Jared asked, "How did you know Doug was in town?"

"I've been tracking him. His name came up in a newspaper article and I got an alert."

"How much money does he owe you?" Sara asked.

China played with the hem of her top as she answered, "About $100,000. Give or take."

Jared realized how lucky he'd got. There was no telling what would have happened to the renovation project with someone like Doug on board. He looked up at Sara's next question.

"Why would you give him that kind of money?"

China shrugged and picked at a piece of lint on her

pleather pants. "Love does stupid things. I should never have trusted him, but I did." She peeked up at Sara, then glanced over at Jared. "You did the smart thing by firing him. He's gotten involved in some bad things." China looked back to Sara. "I know you don't like me because of what Doug did to your sister, but you should know, he told me he was divorced when we met. I wouldn't have gone out with him if I knew about Tasha or the kids. He lied to me. Too bad I didn't learn from the start."

Without another word, China left the office.

As the door closed, Jared turned to Sara. The attorney's shoulders relaxed away from her ears and her chest puffed out as she took a deep breath.

"Remind me to never let Renee take vacation time," said Bill.

"Who's Renee?" asked Jared.

Sara said, "Our receptionist. My nephew doesn't usually answer the phones."

Nodding as if he heard explanations like this every day, Jared tilted his head back to the conference room. "Shall we continue our conversation? After this," he waved a finger in the air indicating everything that just happened, "I definitely need your assistance."

Sara held up her hand.

"Give me a minute. I'll meet you in there." And Jared watched Sara walk down the hall.

Jared's gaze followed Sara until she shut her office door. Then he looked back at the two men who were studying him with interest.

"Well. This has been interesting." Jared looked around the lobby before taking a step toward the hallway. "Well, if you'll excuse me, I guess I'll wait for Sara."

Rich shook his head.

"Why don't we talk first? Fill us in on what you're proposing for Sara."

The man's word choice startled Jared. The situation reminded him of the joke about an overprotective father cleaning his guns at the kitchen table while he waited for his daughter's date to arrive. Jared wondered if he really wanted to date Sara but shook off the thought. While he wanted to escape to the conference room, he turned to deal with Sara's partners.

"As you saw, I'm short a local counsel and a project lead. I've done some research and Sara would be a good fit for the counsel position. I'm sticking with my original pick for project lead, Brad Gerome. That sums it up."

Rich stepped away from the door and stood next to Bill.

"You don't know any of us, and you're about to offer Sara a job. Aren't most corporate lawyers more methodical in their hiring practices?"

The exact thought had crossed his mind earlier and he didn't have a good answer for the attorney. The best he could come up with was that Sara had gotten under his skin in the short time he'd known about her and he was drawn to her for some strange reason. Jared had no intention of telling either Rich or Bill that. It would sound crazier if he said it out loud than it already did in his head. Instead, he calmly explained himself again.

"The Miller Agency is methodical, which is how we ended up with Ron. Since that didn't work out so well, I need another option. Sara fits the bill," he said. "Is there a problem?"

The men looked at each other and Rich nodded at Bill.

"You tell him. I don't want in the middle of this."

Frowning, Jared asked, "In the middle of what?"

"Let me explain something about this town. We may be small, but we are a passionate group of people," said Bill. "The issue is you've riled everyone up. Whether you meant to or not, you hired Doug to fill a position that he has no business in. The local paper reported on it, which brought up some of Doug's past legal troubles which in turn now has everyone on edge. Anything you do from here on out will be closely monitored."

Running his hand through his hair, Jared said, "So are you saying the project is doomed?"

"No, not at all," said Bill. "But I think you need to get out of town and let Sara handle this. If you want this renovation to go smoothly, you need to play by the local rules. You don't have to like them, but you have to obey them."

"Would Sara agree with this?"

"Absolutely. But you need to give her full disclosure on the project. Sara Shaw doesn't let herself get in over her head," Bill said. "And I don't like to see my partner set up for failure. Sara is a great attorney. She knows the law and how to work the law within the confines of this community. But her family is her Achilles heel." Bill looked down the hallway, as if to make sure her office door was still closed. "She wouldn't like me telling you this, but between Tasha and Helene, Sara has had more than her fair share of drama. She doesn't care for it, but she puts up with it because she has to. It has cost her, though."

Jared glanced down the hall as well. Irritated he was becoming as suspicious as the man in front of him he said, "What do you mean?"

"Helene isn't shy about her opinion. She tends to overshare, which doesn't go over well with some people," said Rich. His nose wrinkled. "Those same people believe the apple doesn't fall far from the tree."

"And then you have Tasha, who really is a nice young woman. She married the wrong man, which around here can be an unforgivable sin." Bill sat back on the receptionist's desk. "Although, since Tasha stood up to Doug, she's regaining respect. Dating Greg has helped too."

"Greg?" asked Jared. It occurred to him he'd never learned this much about any of his other local counsel. Hell, he didn't even know this much about his assistant, and she wanted to sleep with him.

"He's Blake's soccer coach. He and Tasha have been dating for a while. Rumor has it that Greg is going to propose."

Rich added, "You know if Brad doesn't want to work on the project, you could ask Greg. He's some sort of project manager. Not sure what sort of architecture experience he has, but I've heard good things about him."

Tucking that bit of information away for future use, Jared said, "I think you two have filled me in on all the gossip I need for now. Maybe even more than I needed to know."

The two men smiled at each other.

"You have no idea what kind of town you've entered, Jared Hughes," said Rich.

Bill nodded. "Don't say we didn't warn you."

19

Sara seethed as she listened to Bill and Rich talk to Jared. How dare they act like overprotective parents. Her mother was bad enough. Sara didn't need anyone else working against her.

When she heard Jared start down the hallway, she hurried to her office and closed the door. Sara wanted a minute to pull herself together before she went to the conference room. Kicking off her shoes, she bent over into downward dog and took long, slow breaths.

The entire day was a mess. Doug's behavior was par for the course, but what the hell made her pull China's hair? That was something other people did but not her. What sort of impression had that made on Jared? She doubted the man wanted her to be his local counsel now.

Her cell phone cut into her thoughts. Tiffany's "I Think We're Alone Now" blasted, and Sara hurried to mute it. Her sister's ringtone was funny, but she didn't want the entire office hearing it. She read the message.

Home safe. Don't give Mom the tapes! Have fun with Jared. Did China leave????

Sara considered her response. Seeing what she exposed her niece and nephew to, she felt bad, but at least they missed the main event. Neither one needed to know happened. And as for giving her sister details about Jared. No way. Texting back, she told her sister,

Tapes are safe. China left. Hope Libby's nose is okay.

She sent the message, then added a second one.

Thanks again for helping. I'm sorry you had to get involved.

Immediately, her sister responded.

No problem. That's what sisters are for.

Tossing her phone back on the desk, Sara shoved her feet into her shoes. Jared was waiting in the conference room and if she didn't get in there soon, Rich or Bill might go in and share more embarrassing stories about her dysfunctional family.

Just the thought of that had her hurrying out of the office and down the hall to the conference room. She raced through the door and slid to a halt when she found Jared sitting at the table.

He smiled and she felt a sense of calm. The man may still think her family was crazy, but he was being nice about it.

"In a hurry?"

She shrugged.

"Didn't want to keep you waiting." She closed the conference room door and made her way to a chair on the opposite side of the table. "You should know that today is a rare occurrence. We don't normally have drama like this in the office. And I've never had to break apart a fight before."

Jared leaned back in his chair. Sara's eyes gravitated back to his mouth which was in an even bigger grin than before.

"Hmm. Based on what your partners were just telling me, I think you've had more than your fair share of drama."

Her calm shattered like a window hit with a baseball. She shouldn't have been shocked, though. Bill and Rich crossed the line.

"I can explain."

Holding up his hand, Jared said, "No need. Between what I saw and what I've heard, I have a clear picture of what Doug is really like. I dodged a bullet when it came to him."

Relaxing back in her seat, Sara said, "Probably." She paused, trying to decide how much information Jared needed.

Might as well tell him everything now, she thought. *It will come up sooner or later.*

"Before we talk about the position, you need to understand a few things."

Jared nodded.

"I'm all ears."

She cleared her throat, stalling for a minute. How could she tell Jared what he needed to know about this town without making herself look the part of the country bumpkin?

And this is why I shouldn't have come home after law school.

Before she could rally her scattered thoughts, Jared rapped his knuckle on the conference table.

"You know what? Let me summarize what I know and then you can fill me in."

Sara motioned for Jared to continue since she didn't know what else to say.

"Your sister's ex-husband lied to me to get a job that he wasn't qualified for. Your ex-brother-in-law's ex-girlfriend lied to you to get a job that she shouldn't ethically take. Your mother oversteps her bounds and your law firm partners resemble overprotective older brothers. And you, for all practical purposes, appear to be caught up in the middle of it all," Jared said. "Does that about sum it up?"

Her face burned with embarrassment. It wasn't like she didn't know all of this already. It was just horrifying that an outsider could see it too. She didn't trust her voice, so she nodded.

"Okay, now that we're on the same page, let's get to business." And just like that Jared launched into an explanation of what he needed for the renovation project. "Oversight is key. I know what I want to do with the building, and I want to use local resources as much as possible. Things tend to run smoother that way. The Miller Agency has been coming into rural locations for the last few years and identifying locations that are both profitable to renovate and beneficial to the community. We need to make money, but the community has to be self-sufficient after we leave. It's a win-win for everyone."

As Jared continued, Sara found herself being drawn into the story he was telling. She didn't know if it was because he was a good salesperson, or because his voice was hypnotic, but she knew she wanted to be involved.

She also knew a smart businesswoman considered all options. When Jared finished going through the details, Sara said, "That sounds like a great project. I've written down several of the other towns where you've done this, and I'll do my research to see how things are going after the fact."

"That's fair," Jared said. He leaned back in his chair again and steepled his fingers in front of his face. "Why do I get the impression there is a "but" coming next?"

"You are very perceptive. You're right. There is a "but". There is always a "but"."

"So?" His blue eyes pinned her to her chair, and she struggled not to squirm under his watch. "What else do you want to know?"

Straightening up in her seat, Sara said, "I want to know what can go wrong. Nothing you said here sounds all that bad. Before I can seriously consider this option, I need to know the downside."

His eyes held hers for a few seconds more, almost too long she thought, before he looked away and nodded.

"Let's see. There's the regular bureaucracy. As local counsel, you'll get to deal with the red tape. Building permits, inspections, that sort of thing. Sometimes the project manager deals with it. But I stay out of that. My responsibility is to make sure the financing comes through. Most of my backers have been with me for years so they trust me and the process." When Jared paused and frowned, Sara sat forward in her chair. "I do have an administrative assistant who thinks she can get me to marry her and a few wannabe investors who hound me on a regular basis, but apart from that, my business life is pretty normal. Nothing like around here."

Sara smiled. He definitely knew how to keep things light.

"Okay. I'll think about it. Give me a couple of days, and I'll get back to you."

Jared extended his hand.

"That's all I can ask."

As his hand enveloped hers, Sara's heart rate speed up. *So much for logical thinking,* she thought as she stood up and showed Jared to the door.

20

Thursday evening, Sara walked into her living room, a bottle of Pinot Grigio in one hand and a wine glass in the other. Setting the bottle and the glass down on the coffee table, she lowered her body to the sofa, tucking her feet under her. She grabbed her favorite blanket. The soft throw comforted her, both physically and mentally. A former client crocheted it for her after Sara handled a really bad divorce.

"Even though my ex is an ass, you made things as nice as you could. I hope this blanket reminds you how much you helped me through this process."

She didn't use the blanket much. Only when she felt like she needed a little extra something to help her calm down. Once she was settled into her nest, she closed her eyes and took a big inhale. Sara counted to four before she blew out that breath to a count of four and repeated the process. She didn't know how long she sat there, but after breathing deeply for so long, she got lightheaded.

"Screw it," she said as she opened her eyes and reached for the wine. She didn't usually drink during the week, but the drama of the last few days had exhausted her so much her normal relaxation techniques didn't work. She'd been to extra yoga classes, stretched for hours, and breathed until she was dizzy. "So much for stress reduction techniques. Bring on the alcohol."

She held the first sip of wine in her mouth and tried to identify the hint of green apple the bottle's label swore she would taste. It tasted like every other wine to her, so she swallowed the cold liquid. Topping off her glass, she grabbed her notepad and settled back in.

After Jared came to her office and went through his proposal for the local counsel position, he'd left her with a decision to make. Did she want to be a local counsel and try something new or did she want the status quo? Sara started writing her pro/con list. It didn't take long to see that the positives of the position outweighed the negatives.

In fact, the only thing that she didn't like was the one little thing Jared neglected to mention in their face-to-face conversation. After Jared emailed the offer letter when he returned to Chicago, Sara found the stipulation. At any time, the local counsel position could be required to transfer to The Miller Agency headquarters.

Taking another sip of her wine, she recalled the conversation she'd had with Jared about the clause.

~

"BUT LOCAL COUNSEL means the attorney stays where she is. Local is local," she'd argued. "If you want someone to move, then it isn't a local counsel position."

"Standard language for all offers," Jared said. "I never know when I'm going to run across an asset for The Miller Agency. We like to be able to keep our options open."

"What about my options? If I sign this as the contract reads, I don't have a choice about moving. And where the hell would I be moving to?"

"Right now, I'm based in Chicago."

Her forehead wrinkled in frustration.

"Right now? Meaning the office could move." She drew a squiggly line with her finger in her Zen sand garden. "Would you sign a contract this open-ended?"

While she waited for his response, she smoothed out the sand.

"It doesn't matter what I would do, Sara. You, of all people, are aware there are no certainties in life. I don't foresee a change in location. But if I put it in writing and something happens, an astute attorney like you would come back at me for breach of contract. Which is precisely why I want you to work for me. You're the kind of powerhouse I need."

～

SWIRLING her wine around in the glass, Sara contemplated Jared's remark. She was a powerhouse, no doubt. But was he flattering her to get what he wanted or was he telling her the truth as he saw it?

She glanced back down at her list. The bump in salary would be nice. She was well paid, but as her mother frequently reminded her, she had law school loans. It would be nice to tell her mother the loans were paid off the next time she suggested Sara ask Tasha for the money. Despite Helene's assertion that Tasha should share her lottery win and would be happy to help out her family, Sara steered clear of the subject. In her opinion, it was a tacky and impolite request, similar to all the others Tasha got on a regular basis. And more importantly, Sara didn't need the help. She was capable of taking care of herself.

But that was one of the many things her mother didn't get. Which made the next pro on her list that much more interesting: working with people outside of her hometown. It would be nice to work on a project that no one else in town knew much about. She could expand her horizons and not worry about things getting back to her mother.

Helping her hometown was another pro. Despite her mother, Sara was proud of what her town stood for. This project would add cash to the town's economy.

But the sole con on the other side of the paper made her pause. Was she okay with the possibility of moving away from the place she had called home for her entire life? Yes, she'd left for college and law school, but she'd come back home because —well, she wasn't really sure why. She'd turned down several offers at some prestigious law firms. Her professors told her she was crazy to do it. In fact, her decision to return home is what finally ended her one and only serious relationship.

Not wanting to revisit that again, Sara doodled in the margin of her paper. She'd done everything she could here. Maybe it was time to see what a bigger market like Chicago had to offer. There wasn't anything in Jared's contract that said she had to stay. If she hated it, she could move back.

But back home, her mother would definitely be waiting for her with a bunch of ridiculous ideas. Thinking about her mother reminded her of the voicemail message she'd listened to earlier.

"Hello, this is Thomas Radcliffe, Relationship Coordinator for Busy Professionals. I'm trying to reach Sara Shaw. Helene Shaw suggested I give you a call to see if there's anything I can do to assist you on your journey to 'couplehood'."

Recalling the message made her snort.

"Who in their right mind says '*couplehood*'?"

Sara hadn't taken the time to call Helene to find out exactly what she'd done. If her mother hired this guy, then her mother could fire him. There was no way Sara was going to get sucked into another one of her schemes.

As soon as the thought crossed her mind, Sara knew what

her best decision was. She needed to be open to the opportunity of getting out of town and starting a life of her own. It was that simple. The small-town life, surrounded by people she'd known since she was in diapers was fine, but it would be nice to branch out and meet new people. Maybe then she wouldn't need a relationship coordinator.

21

The next morning, Sara held the phone to her ear and listened to her client rant about her current situation. She knew from experience that she was a sounding board and nothing she said right now would make a difference. This client didn't seem to care that her complaints were billable, and there was nothing Sara could do.

I'm not a therapist, thought Sara. *Maybe I should suggest she get one. It would be cheaper.*

The rant continued as Sara learned how her client's sister wasn't sure what to do now that she'd moved, and her husband served her with divorce papers.

"I mean what state in its right mind doesn't allow alimony. We all told her she shouldn't leave home. At least here, we could all pitch in. There's no way in hell I'm going to that ass-backwards state."

Not sure what state her client was complaining about, Sara did her best to steer the conversation back to something she could help with.

"Your sister needs to find legal representation in her area. As much as I would like to help you, my hands are tied."

"Damn it, that's what my therapist said," the woman shrieked. "I hate it when she's right."

Wow, thought Sara. I guess the therapist got tired of listening.

"I needed to be sure she was telling me the truth," her client continued. "I don't know what to do now, though. Sissy shouldn't suffer like this."

Sara offered to look up some attorneys and email them to her client. Her client promised to give her an update on the situation, and Sara hung up the phone. Running her hands through her hair, she leaned back and sighed.

She had planned to hint to her client that Rich would be better suited to work with her moving forward but thought better of it. After the direction the conversation went, Sara decided to wait. She hadn't accepted Jared's offer so there was no reason to get her client more ruffled than she already was. But a call to Jared was in order. She was ready to take the job.

Taking a second to regroup, Sara closed her eyes and repeated her most recent mantra, "I accept where I am here and now" to the empty room.

"Why would you want to do that? You're sitting in your office with your eyes closed," said Rich. His statement was followed by the sound of something heavy hitting her desk. "You're about to take on a new role. You should be out celebrating. Oh, by the way, I need your help with these."

Counting to five in her head, Sara kept her eyes closed when she asked, "How do you know I'm taking the role? I haven't decided yet."

"You have decided. You just haven't announced it yet."

Sara knew he was right but refused to let it bother her. Instead she asked, "What did you need my help with?"

"Open your eyes and find out."

Irritated by Rich's interruption, she opened one eye. A two-foot stack of files greeted her. Her other eye flew open.

"Wait a minute," said Sara confused by his actions. "I'm the one taking on a new role. Shouldn't I be giving you my files? Not the other way around."

Easing himself into a side chair, Rich crossed his arms over his chest and stretched out his legs.

"I knew it. You made a decision." Rich winked at her. "No reason to lighten your load because you're taking a local counsel position. Besides, I don't think that's all you want out of this."

Sara froze. She wasn't sure what Rich meant. There was no way he could read her mind and know she was interested in Jared. But he could also be referencing the job. Knowing the only way to find out, she asked, "What do you mean, exactly?"

Rich smirked at her.

"As if you don't know what I'm talking about. You think if you take the local counsel position, you'll attract more clients from the surrounding towns. What else did you think I meant?"

Relieved that Rich was off track, Sara considered his comment. The three partners had their own clients. Even in a small town, there was enough business to go around. She wondered if Rich was jealous, but before she could ask him about it, he changed the subject.

"Bill and I have a bet that when Renee gets back from vacation, she'll talk you out of this."

Knowing he was giving her a hard time, Sara decided to dish it back.

Mirroring his posture, Sara asked, "Why were you in the office to witness China's fight with Doug? I thought you had a trial this week."

Sara recognized the guilt that contorted Rich's face, and he stood up.

Before he could make it to the door, she called to him, "Oh no. You don't get to walk out of here without an explanation. I'd like to know how both you and Bill had front row seats to this mess."

Rich gave Sara what she could only call a sheepish grin and said, "Case settled, so I came back to the office. Good thing too, because once Bill figured out who she was, I didn't want to miss the action."

"Action? Are you telling me you predicted I would be pulling hair and Doug would get decked?" Sara asked. "It was like a soap opera, and I don't even watch them."

"Doug was a bonus. Never thought the guy would show up here. He has quite the set of cojones, doesn't he?"

"He lacks common sense and any ability to follow the law. That's what I think." The rest of Rich's statement registered with Sara. "Wait a minute. With no case, you have plenty of time to take care of these on your own. There is no way I'm going through these files. Do them yourself."

She scooped up the files Rich had dropped on her desk and walked to him. Rich accepted the files with resignation, but she was glad to see he didn't argue with her. As he left her office, he called over his shoulder, "If you won't help me out with filing, don't expect any favors from me."

Relieved he didn't make fun of her mantra Sara went back to work. She glanced down at the notes on her desk. As soon as she found an attorney to help Sissy, she could go through her files and figure out who would be best suited to take over her open cases. Sitting down in her chair, she scrolled through her online address book and made a list of who might be helpful. She'd made it through the "N"s when the phone rang.

"Sara Shaw. How can I help you?"

Jared's voice greeted her before asking, "By starting your new position. I have a pile of files to be reviewed, and I need an architect. I'd prefer Brad, but I'll take whomever you can give me."

22

Sara cleared her throat to give herself a few seconds to figure out how to respond. Jared didn't seem to need her official "yes" based on the fact he was already telling her what to do. The previous evening proved she wanted the position as did her actions this morning, so it was clear what she needed to do. Sara pulled out her notepad and pen.

"Give me a run-down of the files." She waited expectantly to hear exactly what Jared needed her help on. When she didn't get a response, she asked again, "Jared, let's go through the files."

"They're not in front of me at the moment. Walters still has them."

Nodding her head, she sat back in her chair.

"So, am I to understand that my new boss has the proclivity for exaggeration?"

His chuckle made her stomach flutter. Thankful they weren't face-to-face, she realized she would need to get herself under control. Having a crush on her new boss would not do.

"Touché. We do have a lot of work ahead of us. I don't want the transition from Gerome and Walters to slow things down."

"I can get up to speed quickly," Sara assured him. Curiosity made her ask, "Has Doug contacted you again?"

"Three emails and two phone calls. He seems to think having a contract means he can't be fired, so he's been carrying on as if he's still in charge of the project."

Having dealt with Doug before, she was well aware of his behavior when he didn't get what he wanted. She also knew it was better to nip things in the bud with him.

"You did set him straight, though?"

"Of course, though not before he secured a plumber. You can never have too many plumbers," Jared chuckled, but he got serious when he continued. "But I explained to him he is an employee at-will and as a heterosexual, white male in his mid-30s, he has no protections in the current working environment."

"What you're saying is being an asshole doesn't give you any rights?" The question came out of Sara's mouth before she could censor. Jared laughed loudly, causing her to pull the phone away from her ear.

"You are going to be a hell of a lot more entertaining to work with than Ron. That man is dry as a bone," said Jared when his laughter died down. "But just so you know, Doug has no leg to stand on. I wrote the employment contract, so you don't need to worry about him anymore." Jared cleared his throat before he continued. "I take it from this conversation that you're accepting the offer."

She nodded her head even though he couldn't see her.

"Yes. I am."

"Good. Because I would hate to have to rescind the email that should be in your inbox right now." She glanced at her computer and sure enough, an email with the subject line, *Local Counsel Agreement,* was visible. "Can you sign and return that at your earliest convenience?"

"Sure. No problem." Sara put her pen down. "Do you want to table our conversation until I've completed the paperwork?"

"No, we need to get rolling on this. Now that I have a new local counsel and a plumber, I need a project coordinator," said Jared. "I want Brad Gerome."

Sara knew Jared didn't want to hear what she had to say, but it was better that he heard it sooner than later.

"As your local counsel, I don't think that's a good idea."

"Explain your concerns."

The tone of his voice told Sara that Jared switched to full work mode.

At least it will be easy to know if I am dealing with boss Jared or friendly Jared, she thought.

"The fact that he's Doug's brother, though he is well liked and accepted in the community, could pose a few problems." Sara added, "Quite frankly, the fact that I'm Doug's ex-sister-in-law might be a problem as well."

The steel in Jared's voice took Sara aback.

"Doug isn't getting in the way. Call Brad. Present the opportunity. See what he says."

Jared's voice gave her pause. Was this job going to be a bigger pain in the ass than she thought? Jared seemed pretty laid back. He made it through the chaos of China, Doug, and Tasha the other day without a scratch. Did that break him down already? Or was he not what he seemed to be? Her initial impression of a fair but forceful leader might be off. Maybe he was a tyrant who didn't like it when his employees expressed their opinions.

Then again, she thought, *Doug gets on everyone's nerves.*

Wanting to give him the benefit of the doubt, Sara said, "All right. I'll give him a call when we're finished. What else do you have for me?"

"What about China? Did she reach out to you?"

Curious as to why he would be interested, Sara said, "No. I

haven't heard from her. I didn't really expect to, but you never know."

"Is your receptionist back from vacation?" asked Jared.

"Now I get it. You want to know if I'm still doing double duty around here," she said with a smile. "Renee will be back next week. No need for you to worry. We have this under control."

The remainder of the conversation went off without a hitch and when Sara put down the phone, she wondered if she overreacted. Jared had been nothing but pleasant and he was more than generous with the timeline he set for her.

She chewed on her lower lip as she looked over her to-do list. It was manageable but she would need to get started if she wanted to get out of here in time. She promised Blake and Libby she'd come to dinner.

"Might as well get this over with sooner than later," she said as she dialed Brad's office number. "The worst he can say is no."

23

"Yes, I understand, Brad," said Sara as she stared out her office window. She'd expected Brad to decline the offer but hadn't anticipated the reason. "Having a baby is going to be time consuming. I can't believe you and Carlton were able to get matched up with a surrogate so fast. That is amazing news."

Brad's excitement radiated through the phone.

"I know! The agency said we could wait for years but we've only been on the list for a couple of months," said Brad. "We decided not to tell anyone until we knew for sure. Carlton thought we would jinx it if we told too many people."

"You've told Tasha though, right? She'll be thrilled."

"She was! I think the ringing in my ear has stopped from her shrieks," said Brad. "The kids know, too. Carlton and I wanted to include them in all the details. We want them to know they'll still be important to us even though we'll have our own child."

"Don't tell me. Libby volunteered to babysit, right?"

Brad's laugh filled the line.

"Of course, she did. What did you expect? Blake surprised us both, though."

Pulling out her chair, Sara sat down and rested her chin on her palm.

"I take it he wasn't excited."

"Quite the opposite actually. He said he would be happy to be the baby's soccer coach when he or she was old enough to play. Blake said he could work with a boy or girl, so it was okay whatever we have."

Sara chuckled at the thought of Blake having that conversation. The kid was maturing every day. Someday, he would be quite the catch, especially if he took after his uncle.

God help the world if he followed his father's footsteps, she thought.

"All right, I need to come up with plan B. For now, I can handle the legal aspects of things, but I don't have the bandwidth or the knowledge to be able to deal with the building project itself," said Sara. She bit her bottom lip as she thought about her next steps. "Do you have any suggestions?"

"Nothing off the top of my head, but if I think of anything, I'll let you know," said Brad. "Hey, thanks for talking with Carlton about his business set up. He won't admit it, but he was relieved to have you review everything. The minor tweaks you suggested were simple and now he has peace of mind. Especially now that we're starting a family. Neither of us wants to have something happen on the business front that could hurt the family."

A thought crossed her mind.

"Do both of you have a will set up?" asked Sara. "As morbid as it sounds, you need to have things in place in case something happens. Trusts and guardians. And life insurance."

A long sigh came across the line.

"We don't, but that's another thing that needs to be done. Could you help us with that?"

Looking at the list of things on her plate, Sara predicted some late nights in her immediate future. Estate planning documents were easy, and it was the least she could do for Brad, considering all the help he had been to Tasha over the years.

"I'll email you and Carlton the planning documents. Fill them out and get them back to me."

"Thanks, Sara! Good luck finding someone for The Miller Agency."

Noticing her ever growing list, Sara turned to her computer and pulled up the documents she would need from Brad and Carlton. Attaching them to the short email she composed, she hit send. At least that was out of the way.

Frustrated by the fact that she had no idea where to find a project coordinator for Jared, she sat at her desk and thumped her pen against the arm of her chair. Her mind had been fuzzy today and she couldn't quite figure it out. Concentrating was a struggle, but something needed to change and fast.

In an effort to get her brain started, she doodled on her desk pad. She came up with three or four suggestions for the project manager, though none of them excited her. Then it hit her.

Not once today had she done any of her deep breathing exercises or yoga stretches.

The realization that years of healthy habits had been broken due to this new position forced her from her chair. She kicked off her shoes and took a deep breath. She felt the air go into her lungs. Normally, this was when she felt reenergized, but all the air did was make her cough. She took control of herself and tried again. She raised her arms over her head to do a swan dive pose. Halfway down, she lost her balance and tilted toward her desk. She caught the arm of her chair and raised herself up as her head came a few inches from the desk's glass top. Holding on, she bent her knees and plopped down on the floor.

"What the hell is going on with me?"

Sara couldn't remember the last time that yoga hadn't worked to help her calm down and de-stress. It was the only thing through the years that she could count on. Was it a coincidence or did Jared's job offer have bad luck associated with it?

"That's ridiculous," Sara said. Determined, she put her feet straight out in front of her and reached for her toes. Her hamstrings protested, but she held the stretch for the count of thirty. Then to prove to herself that she was only imagining things, Sara stretched further, clasping her hands underneath her feet. Her legs tightened in protest, but she held on, forcing herself to complete the move.

"Damn it! This isn't possible."

"What's not possible?" Bill poked his head in the door. Confusion, then humor crossed his face as he walked in and set his briefcase down. "Did you fall over in downward cat?"

"It's downward-facing dog, and no, I did not." Sara didn't explain it was swan pose that almost gave her a concussion. Rather than try, she brought the bottom of her feet together in front of her and continued to stretch. "Just clearing my head." The thought also occurred to her that both of her partners had stopped into her office unannounced today. "Can I help you with something?"

Bill shook his head.

"No. Just heard you talking to yourself. You're beginning to worry me, Sara. Is the stress getting to you?" He looked down at his watch. "What are you still doing here, anyway? Don't you have yoga class?"

Irritated that Bill decided to pay attention to her schedule today, she straightened out her right leg and leaned over to touch her toes.

"I'm eating dinner with Tasha and the kids tonight. Thought I would get myself stretched out since I'll miss yoga."

Bill gave a short snort before he said, "Okay. Well, you have a good dinner. I'm headed home. When does Renee get back?"

"Monday," she said holding up her hand to interrupt Bill. "Yes, Rich told me about your bet."

"I've got a nice twenty-year-old bottle of Scotch that says you turn Hughes down. Not that you shouldn't take the job, but I don't think Renee is going to be happy with you changing the office dynamics." He grabbed his briefcase and walked to the door. As he left, he said, "Although if she gets a look at Jared, Renee might fight you for the position."

24

Tasha's kitchen looked like a war zone when Sara stepped in. Flour covered the island with pools of red sauce standing out like blood in a battlefield. Blake stood next to the oven, peering in the window, as if willing the pizza to cook faster.

Libby saw her aunt first.

"You made it! Mommy said you were busy today, but we knew you would come." Libby gave her a hug which Sara returned. Libby's eyebrows flew up when she noticed what she was wearing. "Why are you wearing yoga clothes? I thought you were going to hang out with us tonight?"

Her brother turned when he heard Libby. "Yeah, we're gonna watch *Deadpool*. You promised."

"Blake, you know you're not allowed to watch that movie. It will give you nightmares. I know from experience," said Tasha as she came in from the dining room. Her sister frowned at her outfit, but Tasha didn't say anything. "We can watch the dragon show if you want."

Before an argument broke out, Sara said, "I wanted to get

comfy for pizza night, so I put on the workout clothes that I keep in my office. Is that okay?"

Nodding his head, Blake said, "Guess what? I made my own special recipe. You're gonna love it."

Sara looked at her sister and her niece for affirmation. Tasha shrugged and Libby stuck out her tongue. So much for positive reviews. Her stomach growled, reminding her she missed lunch.

Hearing the noise, Blake pointed to the pantry. "There're snacks if you're hungry. It's gonna be a couple of minutes before this is ready."

"That's sweet of you, Blake, but I'll be okay."

She saw his shoulders drop and wondered why he was upset.

"Blake, I told you. No more cookies before dinner. Don't you dare try to make Aunt Sara an accessory to the crime." Tasha's hands rested on her hips. "You should know better by now."

Glad to know she didn't have anything to do with his disappointment, Sara waited for the inevitable question.

"What's 'an accessory to the crime'?" asked Blake. The oven timer sounded before anyone could answer, and Blake grabbed the potholders from the cabinet. "It's ready!"

"You don't know that for sure," Libby corrected him. "You have to make sure the cheese melted, and the crust is golden."

Sara walked over to where her sister was standing and listened as the kids bickered about how to tell when the pizza was ready.

"Thanks for having me for dinner," she said to Tasha. "Sorry I'm late."

Tasha waved off the apology.

"You've got a lot going on." Tasha surprised her with a quick hug and then squealed. "I'm so excited for you! A job offer with the bonus of a cute boss!"

Returning the hug, Sara said, "I accepted the job, but yes, the boss is cute."

Tasha winked as she asked, "Have you told Mom yet?"

A wave of irritation hit Sara. It wasn't Tasha's fault for asking, but Sara didn't want to think about Helene's reaction. Her father, Max, would be supportive. He never questioned her choices. But Helene never seemed to understand that she was capable of making her own decisions. Which reminded her of the relationship coordinator she hadn't called back.

Holding her sister at arm's length, Sara said, "Have you ever heard the phrase 'couplehood' before? I'm not sure what that's supposed to mean."

Tasha shrugged. "I think there was a book by that name. Some actor wrote it. Is that what you're talking about?"

Before they could finish their conversation, Blake yelled, "Pizza's ready! I'm taking it out of the oven."

"You don't have to yell," said Libby. "Mom and Aunt Sara are standing right there."

"Don't touch it!" called Tasha, as she hurried to the oven to oversee the process. "We don't need any third-degree burns tonight. Aunt Sara is an attorney, not a doctor."

Sara leaned back on the counter and let her mind wander as she watched the commotion. It was nice to not be in charge every once in a while. While she didn't want to do this every night, it was relaxing to let someone else take over things.

While the kids continued to bicker over who pulled the pizza from the oven, the doorbell rang.

"I'll get it," said Sara, turning toward the living room. "Are you expecting someone?"

"It's probably Greg. He said he would drop by and see how things turned out. I hope that's okay."

"Sure, no problem." Sara kept the disappointment from her voice as she prepared to open the door. She liked her sister's boyfriend, but she valued her time with her family alone.

Pasting a smile on her face, she opened the front door. The smile fell from her face as she saw China standing on the front porch.

Sara hurried out the door, closing it firmly behind her. Looking over her shoulder to make sure no one followed her, she shooed China from the porch to the front steps where they'd be harder to see from the window. Sara's forehead scrunched together as she stared at the woman in front of her.

"What are you doing here?"

China opened her mouth to speak, then closed it again. Not sure what to do next, Sara asked, "Are you okay? What is going on?"

"I came to see Tasha," said China. She pulled at the hem of her shirt.

Sara asked, "How did you know where Tasha lived?"

China rolled her eyes.

"I thought attorneys were smarter than that," said China. "While Doug and I were dating, I mailed all of the kids' birthday cards and presents. Tasha's address is in my phone. I never took it out. Did you really think Doug took the time to send things to his kids?"

Irked by her oversight, Sara glanced over her shoulder and peered up at the living room window. No one had followed her to the door, but it was only a matter of time before someone got curious about who was at the door. She took a deep breath to calm herself and turned back to Doug's ex.

"What do you want?"

China cleared her throat.

"I came to tell Tasha I was sorry. I figured the kids would be in bed and I could tell her myself," said China, giving Sara a half smile. "I didn't know Doug was married when we got together. By the time I found out, it was too late. She doesn't have to believe me, but it's the truth. That's it. And since it's clear you aren't going to let me talk to her, I'll leave."

China turned around and walked down the sidewalk.

"Wait," Sara surprised herself when she called out. China turned around and for the first time, Sara realized the woman wore the same outfit as before, only this time her matted hair gave the impression of not being washed for several days and her clothes were wrinkled. Her make-up had been touched up, but the dark circles under her eyes couldn't be hidden. Curious, Sara asked, "Where have you been the last few days? I thought you'd be back in Saint Thomas by now."

Looking around as if she expected Doug to pop up, China said, "I'm not going back there. It's over between Doug and me, and I want as far away from him as possible. I found a job in Las Vegas."

Leery that she was being played, Sara studied the woman in front of her. China was a smart person who could take care of herself. Though she hadn't met her before this week, she had heard plenty from her sister and her mother.

The problem was the woman in front of her didn't match the description of what she had heard over the years. This woman appeared down on her luck, not the mistress who ruined her sister's marriage. Shaking her head, Sara suspected this was what China wanted her to think. From what she knew, China knew how to manipulate people and Sara wouldn't fall prey to that.

"Then why are you still in town? You've spent a week in a town you hate, for a job you're overqualified for, that you only worked at for an hour. There has to be something else."

"I needed money to get out of here. Trust me, I would have left sooner if I could have." China pushed her hair behind one ear. "The temp agency had another job, which I finished today. I've got enough to get me to Vegas. My bus leaves tomorrow, but I thought...no I needed to tell Tasha I'm sorry."

"Why didn't you say something when you were in the office?"

The woman's face crumbled. "I didn't know how. Everything happened so fast and when Tasha showed up, I knew it looked bad." She rubbed away the tears on her face with the palms of her hands. "Look, I just wanted to tell Tasha the truth. I'm sorry for what happened, but it wasn't my fault. Doug is—"

Tasha interrupted, "a douche."

Sara whipped around to see her sister standing on the porch.

"How much of that did you hear?" she asked.

"Enough. I always wondered what he told you. Or didn't, as it turned out." Tasha gave China a tight smile before she looked at Sara. "Dinner's ready and you weren't back. I'm glad I didn't send Libby or Blake out. Blake threatened to karate chop China if she showed again."

China returned Tasha's smile. "That sounds like Blake." She put her hand to stop Tasha from speaking. "Look, I'm glad you heard what I said. Trust me, I really am sorry. No one deserves what you went through. I should have come clean on Monday, but I didn't expect to be assigned to Sara's office. And I sure as hell didn't expect you to show up. I'll leave now."

China turned, and Sara walked to the porch and stood by Tasha. Her sister leaned her head on her shoulder as they watched China walk down the street.

"I never saw that coming," said Tasha. "How could I have been so wrong about her?"

Pulling her sister back to the door, Sara shrugged. "Some people aren't what they seem." She elbowed her sister. "Come on. Let's go eat some pizza."

25

As Tasha walked back into the house with her sister, Libby's voice called out, "Mom! We need you in the kitchen!"

Tasha glanced at her sister before running back to the kitchen.

A white haze shrouded the room. As she peered through the fog, she saw Blake wiping flour off the kitchen cabinet directly onto the floor.

"What in the world are you doing, Blake? That isn't how we clean the kitchen."

Her son froze, his arm poised over another pile of flour that would soon find its way to the floor. Quickly recovering from being caught, he picked up more flour and threw it in the air.

"It's snowing, Mom! Isn't it awesome? I get to play in the snow but not wear those scratchy snow pants."

Before she could come up with a response, Sara bumped into her.

"What the hell happened in here? I wasn't outside that long."

Libby shook her head at her aunt. "You can't say bad words, Aunt Sara. It isn't polite."

"It's snowing, Aunt Sara! Isn't it cool?" Blake bent down and picked up the flour that fell to the floor. He scooped up a handful and threw it in the air, ducking under it so the white powder coated his hair as it floated back to the ground. "See? It's just like snow, but it's not cold."

Taking control of the situation, Tasha ordered, "Blake, walk out to the backyard and dust yourself off. Do not walk back into this house until there isn't a drop of flour on your body."

As Blake headed out the door, Tasha gave Libby one of her patented "Please can you help your brother out of this mess" smiles. Without a word, Libby nodded and followed him. With the kids out of the room, Tasha slumped against the doorframe.

"You're getting flour on your shirt, you know," said Sara.

Crossing her arms over her chest, Tasha's eyes narrowed as she said, "I'll deal with it. I need a minute to recover from the conversation outside. Tell me what's going on."

The edge of Sara's mouth twitched.

"Well, I wasn't standing here, but my guess is that Blake accidentally knocked some flour over and decided it looked like snow." Sara gestured around at the room with a hint of a smile on her face. "The rest is history."

Pointing a finger at her sister, Tasha said, "That's not what I was talking about and you know it."

Sara held out her hands as if to make a peace offering.

"We can do a postmortem on the apology after dinner. I think you've got bigger issues right now."

Tasha walked to the pantry and grabbed a broom. Handing it to Sara, she said, "We can talk about it after you clean up this mess." When Sara started to protest, Tasha put her disappointed-mom face on and said, "If you hadn't been outside so long, this wouldn't have happened. Now, clean it up while I check on the kids."

∼

Long after the pizza mess was cleaned up and the kids were tucked into bed, Tasha poured her sister a cup of coffee.

"Let me get this straight ... China wanted to apologize to me for not knowing Doug was married." Tasha rubbed her temples. "And her showing up in your office was a coincidence. Why do you suppose she got so upset with Doug then? Punching him in the face isn't really a form of apology I've heard of before."

Shrugging, Sara said, "Doug makes everyone mad. And she wasn't apologizing to him. Only to you. I suspect she'd haul off and deck him again if she were given a chance. Especially since she has to take the bus to Vegas."

Tasha took a sip of coffee before she said, "That will be a sight to see. I'm glad I'm not the passenger sitting next to her."

Sara winked. "Me too! But at least we know she doesn't have anything to do with what's going on here."

"Speaking of which," Tasha asked what was really on her mind, "How's the new job going? Curious minds want to know."

Sara adjusted the magazines that were sitting on the coffee table so that the corners were in perfect alignment. For as long as she could remember, Sara organized things when she was upset or avoiding something.

"OCD, much?" Tasha asked, grinning at the look her sister gave her. "I'm sorry, but I don't think you can make those any straighter. You're only fiddling so you don't have to answer my question."

Sitting back on the sofa, Sara grabbed her coffee and finished it.

Hmm, thought Tasha. *She's rattled. Or she likes my new coffee blend.*

"I'm not sure the job was such a good idea."

"Of course, it was. You wouldn't have accepted unless your

pro/con spreadsheet agreed." Her sister's cheeks flushed. "You don't make decisions like that unless you've thoroughly evaluated the opportunity."

Sara blew air out of her mouth, making a farting sound Blake would be jealous of. "You are correct, but you're also scary."

Tasha frowned.

"I'm stating the facts. How is that scary?"

"You weren't always this mature. My little sister has grown up," said Sara. "But it's nice to have someone to bounce ideas off. If only you knew someone who needs a job overseeing a building project."

Picking up the empty coffee cups, Tasha stood up and started toward the kitchen. "Too bad Brad is going to be busy with a baby. He would've been perfect for this."

She walked into the kitchen and added the cups to the dishwasher. Tasha headed back to the living room but paused outside the kitchen door when she saw Sara sitting on the couch, her eyes closed. Something was off tonight. Sara wasn't herself. Her sister had arrived wearing yoga clothes and not once had she done any yoga. Tasha needed to get to the bottom of things.

While she contemplated her best approach, Tasha continued their conversation about Brad. "It's hard to believe that Brad and Carlton are going to be parents. I'm happy for them, but I wonder if they have any idea what they're in for."

"Did you?" asked Sara, keeping her eyes closed.

"No. Not in the slightest," said Tasha sitting across from her sister. "If someone told you all the crap you would go through as a parent, no one would have kids. That's why parents only share the good things their kids do. They don't want to spoil the illusion."

When Sara didn't respond, Tasha reached out and tapped her on the shoulder.

"Are you all right? New job already getting to you?"

Sara opened her eyes and shrugged her shoulders.

"Jared wants Brad. Brad's not available."

"So you've said. Just explain that to Jared. You've given people worse news before," said Tasha. "Speaking of which, did you ever call the relationship coordinator?"

"How is that bad news?"

"Well, if you need your mother's help to get a date..."

The snide remark earned Tasha a rude gesture.

"Whatever. I don't have time to date. I need to concentrate on finding someone for Jared," said Sara. The choice of words struck Tasha as odd. She started to comment Sara could kill two birds when the doorbell rang. "That's probably Greg. You said he was stopping by."

"I was wondering when he would get here," said Tasha, making a mental note to return to the subject of Jared as a dating option once the project came to a close before a thought occurred to her. "China wouldn't come back, would she?"

Running her hands through her hair, Sara said, "I don't think so. She said her peace. But to be safe, be sure you know who it is before you open the door."

"Well, duh," Tasha said as she walked to the door and looked out. Greg grinned back at her, his hands behind his back. "Um, it's Greg. I may need you to leave."

Sara snorted. "Booty call?"

Tasha pushed any embarrassment she might have down and called over her shoulder, "You're jealous. But you too could have a booty call. All you have to do is chat with the relationship coordinator."

Before Sara could retort, Tasha opened the door. "Well, it's about time!"

She leaned in to give Greg a quick peck on the cheek, but Greg wrapped her in his arms and pulled her toward him. Tasha saw his smile before his lips covered hers and she forgot about anything else. It wasn't until she heard a cough that she remembered Sara.

"Hello, Greg. Nice to see you, too," called Sara, and Tasha felt her cheeks heat up.

"Sorry. I didn't realize your sister was still here," Greg said as he gave her a more chaste kiss, then handed her a single white rose.

Taking his hand, Tasha closed the door and pulled him into the living room.

"Come on in. We were just discussing Sara's problem." When her sister sat up straight and glared at her, Tasha realized Sara misunderstood. "She has an open position on the renovation project. Do you know someone looking for a temporary position?"

Her boyfriend sat in an armchair, pulling her onto his lap. Once he had her snuggled the way he wanted, Greg turned to Sara. "I'd be happy to help. What do you need?"

After a brief recap of The Miller Agency's needs, Greg nodded. "This is a temp position with a variety of duties, no set hours, and no possibility of long-term employment. No wonder Doug jumped at it."

"It isn't glamorous, but it pays well," agreed Sara.

Tasha couldn't help adding, "That and he got to hang out around here and make trouble. Win-win for him."

Greg grabbed her hand and kissed it.

"That Hughes guy sent him packing, so don't worry about him anymore." Turning back to Sara, Greg asked, "How much architectural experience do you really need? I know a couple of guys who do construction. They might be able to oversee things, but they wouldn't be able to do much in the way of planning." Putting her hand on his leg, Greg pulled his cell phone out of his pocket. Tasha watched as he scrolled through his contacts. "I could make some calls and see what I can come up with."

Sara's shoulders visibly relaxed, which told Tasha her sister was more concerned about the situation than she let on. Greg's offer was a relief. Tasha thought of several ways to thank him as soon as her sister left.

"That would be great. Thanks for taking the time to help." Sara stood up, grabbed the briefcase she brought in earlier. Tasha started to tell her sister goodnight, but Sara turned back to Greg. "Random thought: would you be interested in taking the position? You understand what's needed. I know you have a job already, but this could be something on the side."

Tasha looked at her sister in surprise.

"Why didn't we think of that earlier?"

Greg looked at her and Sara.

"This is what you've been talking about all night? I figured you'd played games with the kids and complained about your mother," said Greg. He turned to Tasha. "Did you ask her how the relationship thing was going? Max was pretty sure she wouldn't call the guy back." He shrugged at Sara. "I agreed with him. Hope that's okay?"

Waving off his remark, Sara said, "I haven't called the guy back. Probably won't either."

"Helene's not going to like that," Greg said as he smiled. "Enjoy that conversation."

Hoping to get the conversation back on track so she could get Sara out of her house, Tasha tugged on Greg's hand. "Is it something you're interested in? Can you swing another client?"

He kissed her hand, and she felt tingles go down her spine.

"Let me think about it. I wrapped up two contracts last week and my new projects don't start for a couple of months. I haven't done anything like this before, but it sounds interesting."

"I'd like to be able to tell Jared this is resolved," said Sara. "I don't have a lot of options."

"I'm the Hail Mary?"

Tasha rolled her eyes at Greg's humor.

"She didn't mean that." Tasha glanced at her sister. "Or did you?"

"Why would I refer to Greg as a long shot? I need this project to succeed as much as anyone."

Surprised at her sister's knowledge of football, Tasha turned to Greg. "You sure you want to do this? You'd have to work with my sister, you know? She can be a pain in the ass sometimes."

"I am not," Sara said. She laughed and added, "Okay, maybe every once in a while. Greg, I'll email you the information. Look it over and let me know. The Miller Agency has final say, but I think you could do this." Picking up her briefcase, Sara headed to the door. "Goodnight."

Tasha followed her sister and gave her a hug goodbye. "I'm glad you joined us tonight."

Her sister nodded and waved goodbye to Greg who had followed them. As the door closed, Tasha felt Greg's hand rest on her hips, and he kissed her neck.

"Are you really sure you want to do this?" asked Tasha relaxing back into his chest. "I'm not kidding when I say Sara can be a taskmaster."

Greg turned her so she was looking up into his eyes. For a minute, she forgot her question. Standing there with him seemed more important than their conversation.

"I'll think about it." Her heart sped up when he pulled her closer. "Now, I didn't come over her to talk about your sister."

As their lips touched, all thoughts of her sister and the potential job vanished.

26

"You're kidding me! I'm gone for a week, and you take a new job?" Renee's shriek filled the lobby. She whirled around to glare at Rich and Bill. "You two let her do it. And to top it all off, I miss a fight in the lobby with China and Sara. Why is it when I'm here nothing happens and when I leave, I miss everything?"

Sara watched Bill pull out his wallet and hand Rich some money. Before she could ask, Renee started in again. "You made a bet on it, didn't you? I should get a cut of whatever it is."

Shaking her head, Sara let Bill explain himself while she sat back and watched. It felt like Renee had been gone for a month. The receptionist's lack of professionalism needed to be addressed, but that could wait. Sara was glad to have Renee back. As long as the office was running smoothly again, that was the main thing.

The quiet lobby caught her attention, and she noticed that Renee, Bill, and Rich were staring at her.

"What? Did I miss something?" she asked.

"See. Off in her own little world," Rich said.

Bill nodded his agreement. "Renee, you've got your work

cut out for you. It's not only me and Rich you need to keep organized. Sara needs your help, too."

"What?" Sara asked as the men walked out of the lobby. "Where are you going?"

Sara turned back to Renee, who had a grin painted across her face. Sara asked, "What are you smiling about? Everything is the same as before. I don't know what you people are talking about."

"I've known you for years and never once have you got into a physical fight with anyone. Verbal. Yes. But hair pulling? No. And I looked up Jared Hughes online. You neglected to mention your new boss is hot."

Sara felt her cheeks get warm as she turned and headed back to her office, Sara called over her shoulder, "You know, I bet China would be happy to take over the front desk."

Sara smiled as she shut her office door on Renee's protests.

~

THIS WORKLOAD MIGHT KILL *me after all,* Sara thought.

Her neck ached from looking down at the documents that seemed to have multiplied on her desk. It wasn't the renovation project either. Somehow, all her clients wanted something at the same time. She even had an email from Brad. He and Carlton had completed the estate planning questionnaire she had sent them and wanted to schedule a meeting as soon as possible.

"Having a baby really gets people moving," said Sara to herself. "Maybe I should try it."

The thought of gaining thirty pounds, waking up at all hours of the night to pee, and paying day care fees for years was more than enough to scare her out of being a mother. No, being an aunt was the better option. She got to see all the good stuff that happened without dealing with stretch marks and an overactive bladder.

"Okay, focus now. This work isn't going to get finished by itself."

She'd got three paragraphs into Brad and Carlton's questionnaire when she heard a knock at the door. Before she could answer, the door flew open and Helene glided in.

"Good afternoon, Mother," said Sara, wondering if her thoughts on parenthood set off some sort of trigger, beckoning her mother to visit. It reminded her of a reverse Bat-Signal: everything is fine, then *wham*, Helene shows up. "I'm surprised Renee didn't call back when you got here."

"She offered, but I wanted to surprise you." Sara admired the white silk shirt and tan plaid trousers her mother wore. She should ask where Helene got them, if the conversation allowed. When her mother sat down in one of the guest chairs and pulled a legal pad from her purse, Sara doubted they would make it to shopping tips. "You owe me some answers."

Sara waved her arms around the desk.

"Not sure you noticed, but I do have things to do."

Helene's eyes narrowed and she pursed her lips as she took in the desk.

"Hmm. Things do seem a bit messier than usual." Shaking her head, Helene reached over and pulled a pen from Sara's desk. "But you can still make time for your mother, I'm sure."

"Be sure to give that pen back," Sara said. Knowing it was best if she gave into her mother's interrogation, she set a timer on her phone. "You have four minutes to ask me whatever it is you came here to find out. After that, I need to get back to work."

Her mother's nostrils flared slightly. Helene was not happy about being on a schedule.

Serves her right, showing up without calling, thought Sara.

Helene looked down at her notepad, and Sara found herself

studying the top of her mother's head. The perfectly executed highlights hid the gray hairs Helene denied existed. The mix of blond and auburn seemed unusual for her mother, but Sara didn't dare ask. Helene could be persnickety about hair color.

"I can feel you looking at my hair, and I don't have time to explain it," her mother said without looking up.

"How do you do that?" Sara asked. Even as an adult, she couldn't get away with anything. It was a mystery to her how Helene and Tasha could see things without looking. Maybe she should ask Libby. Her niece might know. "It's creepy."

"A secret of parenting. Have a child, and I'll tell you."

Recalling her thoughts on parenthood, Sara said, "That's not happening. What do you want to know? And you have three minutes left." Her mother's head flipped up and Sara found herself looking into her mother's annoyed glare. Sara shrugged. "What? I'm only keeping on schedule."

Helene's chin raised a fraction of an inch, but Sara knew what it meant. *Thin ice ahead. Tread carefully.* Despite being an adult and a lawyer, Helene was her mother and still in charge.

"Okay. What can I help you with?" Sara asked as pleasantly as possible.

Helene crossed her legs, placed the pad of paper on her thigh, and leaned over so that her elbow was resting next to the paper. If the situation wasn't already tense, Sara would've made a crack about channeling Barbara Walters, but she didn't think her mom would respond well. Helene despised Barbara's hairstyle, and based on her new hair color, Sara didn't want to open Pandora's box on the necessity of a good hairdresser.

"Is it true that you took the local counsel position with The Miller Agency and that Jared Hughes is your boss?"

Sara sat up a little straighter.

Starting easy, huh?

"Yes. Effective immediately."

Helene made a note on her sheet before glancing up at the

piles of files on Sara's desk. "Hence all the paper." She frowned. "This group isn't environmentally conscious. If they were, there wouldn't be so many dead trees sitting on your desk."

Surprised by her mother's change of subject, Sara shrugged. "I'll see what I can do. Remember it took me some time to get this firm to make everything digital. Patience."

"It's sad really," said Helene, making another note on her paper. "Libby and I discussed it the other day. She's fearful climate change will ruin her life."

Making a mental note to chat with her niece about what could be done to help the environment, Sara motioned for her mother to continue.

"No need to be rude. I know. I'm on a schedule." Helene cleared her throat. "These next few are yes or no questions. They should be quick."

"Did Jared fire Doug?"

"Yes."

"Did Jared fire Ron Walters?"

"Yes."

"Did Jared get upset with you when Brad said he couldn't take the job?"

Sara shrugged.

"He wasn't happy, but I don't think he was upset. Wait a minute. How did you know Brad didn't take the job?"

A smile covered Helene's face.

"Carlton told me about the surrogacy plan when I got my last adjustment. They're over the moon. I keep telling them that parenting is harder than it looks, and they need to pace themselves. But they're too excited to listen." She leaned forward as if whatever she had to say next was a secret. "They asked Max and me to be the baby's surrogate grandparents."

Scratching her head, Sara asked, "What does that mean exactly?" An image of her mother waddling around pregnant with Brad and Carlton's baby flashed into her head. She blinked a few times, praying the image wasn't seared into her memory. "Please don't tell me you're having this baby for them."

"God no! This isn't *The Jerry Springer Show*, young lady," Helene admonished Sara. "We plan to act as grandparents, that's all. We'd do what we do with Libby and Blake. Take them to dinner, have sleepovers. Spoil them, then return them home. All the fun and none of the responsibility."

Sara joked, "Are you planning to give them unsolicited parenting advice like you do with Tasha?"

"Of course. That is every grandparent's right. Besides, Brad's parents aren't the least bit interested. They've done nothing with Libby and Blake for as long as I can remember. I heard at Bunco that Brad's mother spread some rubbish that Libby and Blake weren't even Doug's children."

Sara rolled her eyes. "Well, that's crap and everyone knows it. Can we get back to the point please?"

"Where was I?" Helene muttered as she squinted down at her page. Sara wondered if she would finally see her mother wearing a pair of reading glasses, but Helene asked her next question without any help. "Did China show up on Tasha's doorstep and ask for money?"

She closed her eyes for a second before letting out a sigh.

"How did you find out about that?"

Her mother smiled and said, "Yes or no, please. I'm on the clock."

Wondering again how her mother was so well informed, Sara said, "Yes, she did. No, she didn't ask for money. She's currently on her way to Las Vegas"

The timer went off before Helene could ask anything else. Sara silenced the buzzing and motioned to her desk. "Time's up. Thanks for coming by, but I need to get back to work."

Helene stood up and tucked the notepad back in her bag. She put the pen on Sara's desk and walked to the door.

Normally, Sara would be impressed by her mother's self-restraint, but she had a feeling that Helene wasn't quite finished.

Sure enough, her mother stopped at the door.

"Final question."

Sara sighed and put her head down on her desk. "Mother, I'm working."

Her head whipped up at the sound of her mother's shriek.

"Have I not taught you proper skincare? Do not rest your face on anything. Wrinkles and lines don't come out of skin, not to mention the myriad of germs that are crawling all over that desk." Helene reached into her purse and pull out a package of wipes. "At least wipe down the part where your forehead is. And don't complain to me when you get stuck with age marks."

Taking the offered wipes, Sara placed them beside her computer.

"I know you aren't leaving until you ask your final question, so go ahead. Shoot."

A Cheshire cat grin appeared on Helene's face. Sara knew she wasn't going to like what came next.

"Yes or no. You called the relationship coordinator back?"

Groaning, Sara regretted giving her mother a final question. She took a deep breath and shook her head.

"I didn't think so," said Helene. "Since that's the case, I'll handle it for you. Have a lovely day, dear. Don't work too hard."

As soon as Helene sauntered out the door, Sara put her head back down on the desk. Family was exhausting. Maybe she should ask Jared to move her to Chicago. At least then she might get some work done.

27

Sara moved the empty food container as she sorted through paperwork. Three months into the renovation project and most of her meals were now eaten at her desk. Tonight's plan of Chinese food worked, except for the fact that the shrimp fried rice had spilled on the new blueprints Jared sent over. She'd brushed off the food as quickly as possible, but not before several stains appeared.

"Appropriate that the house of Wong would have grease on its front door," she said.

Jared would notice the marks. He seemed to notice everything. At first it was a good thing. It was nice to work with someone who knew exactly how much time went into a project. Bill and Rich tended to oversimplify things. They appreciated the work she did, but they never understood how much effort she put in.

Nor did they push her to do better. They'd always let her do her own thing. She'd been her own source of motivation.

With Jared, it was different. His observations were a double-edged sword. Jared demanded perfection on top of accuracy. At first, it was motivating, but Sara learned how exhausting it could be.

Her mother's words echoed in her head, "Be careful what you wish for. You might get it."

She cringed at the thought. Not only was her mother right, this was exactly what Sara used to tell her own clients.

Does this mean I'm becoming my mother? she thought. Shuddering, she pushed the idea aside. Helene was such a busybody, always trying to influence people and get them to do exactly what she wanted. Sara had to admit that sometimes it worked.

Tricking Tasha into speed dating was a good thing, recalled Sara, feeling a bit of envy bubble up. Tasha and Greg were happy together. She knew it from seeing them together as well as listening to Greg on a daily basis. Turned out Greg was a great project manager. He kept the renovations at the waterfront on schedule, bringing issues to her attention only when it was something out of his control. He also dropped in news about his relationship with Tasha. During their last conversation, Greg let it slip he'd asked Max for Tasha's hand in marriage.

"You know, you don't have to do that," Sara had said. "It seems old-fashioned if you ask me. She doesn't need Dad's permission. Or Mom's for that matter."

Greg had shrugged. "I know, but the marriage affects Max and Helene, and they were happy to be included in the process. It's important to get the kids' buy-in, too, so I'm asking both of them. Not to marry me, but to be part of my family with their mom."

"What are you going to do if they say no, they don't want you to marry Tasha?"

"Your mother asked the same thing," said Greg. "But it will be fine. Blake and Libby want this as much as I do."

Thinking back to the conversation, Sara hoped Greg was right. She wouldn't want Greg's plans overruled by two seven-year-olds. But more upsetting was that once again, she and her mother had voiced the same concern. They were more alike than she would like.

Until recently, Sara ignored the similarities, but it was becoming more and more apparent that she was definitely her mother's daughter. It was cringeworthy to think the one person she worked hard to escape was the person she was becoming.

Sara didn't have the energy to deal with her mother issues now, so she shook the thought from her head and turned to shut down her computer. Before she could power down, though, she noticed an email from *The Gazette, announcing its latest articles.* Sara sighed. As much as she wanted to go to home, it was her responsibility to stay on top of local news. So far, the waterfront project had been well received by the town. She clicked on the link in the email and hoped for the trend to continue.

As soon as she saw the headline on the article, Sara's heart sank.

Favoritism hampers renovation
By Cynthia Anderson
Gazette reporter

THE MILLER AGENCY'S *renovation project is in jeopardy according to Gazette sources. With former resident Doug Gerome being replaced by Greg White, a self-employed consultant and current boyfriend of Gerome's ex-wife, sources say other local vendors and contractors have been excluded from working on the project.*

Michael Seaton, managing partner of Davis Investments, went on record with The Gazette.

"Doug was asked to step away from the project," said Seaton. "He

was given no rationale, although The Miller Agency switched local counsel, which may have had an impact."

Since Davis Investments has invested money in the renovation, Seaton indicated he's monitoring the situation for the benefit of his firm and other clients. Concerns are ongoing that the project is not proceeding as planned.

"No one wants to lose money on this," said Seaton.

Mayor Nicole Pilchard expressed her concern about the personnel changes.

"That area of town has a lot of potential to bring jobs and much needed residential and commercial space to the city," said Pilchard. "There is no one better to lead the project than Mr. Gerome."

Several businesses that The Gazette contacted added their concern about the project.

"The Miller Agency is an outside agency who doesn't really care what happens to our community. It is more interested in generating money, regardless of how it will impact the city," said Ron Walters, a local attorney. "Look at how they've treated the locals they did hire. Didn't even leave them in the position long enough to get anything done."

Joe Brown, owner of Joe's Gym echoed Walters.

"The money for this project is private. The city can't really direct the project if the financing is controlled by someone else. It's like letting a kid loose in the candy store."

The Gazette reached out to Sara Shaw, partner at Smith, Rogers & Shaw, LLC and local counsel for The Miller Agency. At the time of this publication, Shaw had not responded.

"WHAT REQUEST?" Sara slammed her hands down on the desk. If Cynthia had bothered to contact her, she would have put this ridiculous theory to rest.

And who the hell was Michael Seaton and Davis Investments? Jared never mentioned he had other backers for this project. She pounded the desk again in frustration. Tomorrow would be spent doing damage control.

Her desk phone rang. Sara sighed when she recognized Jared's cell phone number. Apparently, damage control started now.

28

Taking a deep breath, Sara grabbed the receiver. "Good evening, Jared."

"You're working late."

Stifling a retort that his project was the reason she was still at the office, she plastered a smile on her face. Jared might not be able to see her, but she read somewhere that facial expressions came through in the tone of voice. Her boss didn't need to know her level of exhaustion and irritation.

"Getting organized for tomorrow." Glad he couldn't see her messy desk or tired expression, Sara asked, "What can I do for you?"

"For someone who's in her twelfth hour of work, you sound pretty perky."

"Fourteenth, but who's counting?" she mumbled before it clicked what he said. "Perky isn't something I'm normally accused of being."

"Well, okay then. The reason I called. *The Gazette* dropped an article tonight." She should have known. Jared followed all the news about the renovation, as well he should. "I meant to tell you she contacted me a few times, but of course, I never commented. She made me uncomfortable."

You and every other man within a twenty-mile radius, thought Sara. While Cynthia was usually a reliable reporter, the article made more sense now. "I knew she hadn't contacted me."

"Sorry about that," Jared added, "but there's something else we need to address."

Nodding her head, "I'd say Michael Seaton is the elephant in the room."

"And you would be right. As you know, Davis Investments has no money in this project. I blacklisted them. Years ago. Michael has a bad reputation, and no one in their right mind would do business with him."

"That's good news." Sara relaxed and made a note. "I'll work that into the retraction request to the newspaper and—"

Jared interrupted, "Unfortunately, your predecessor was not in his right mind. He and Doug entered into an agreement with Michael."

A sinking feeling replaced her calm.

"Oh."

"Yeah. Apparently, Doug and Ron agreed to something before I fired them, but never bothered to tell me about it. We can work our way through it, but it makes things more complicated."

Sara grabbed the folder she'd gotten from Ron months ago. "I didn't see anything from him when I went through Ron's files. How did I miss it?"

Her computer beeped to indicate an incoming email.

"I emailed you the file," said Jared. "Michael sent it to me earlier this afternoon. I wasn't sure what he intended to do with it until I saw the article. He wants in on the project and will tank it if he doesn't get his way."

"I'm not going to let that happen," said Sara as she downloaded the file. "Let me review it and I'll get back with you on how we should move forward. I can get the retraction request done, too."

"You should focus on the retraction first. I don't want the town thinking you aren't promoting their best interests." Jared continued, "It makes you look like you don't trust the community. That's not the image I want. Make sure you have time for damage control. Angry citizens aren't good for business. You know better than I do that this work is bringing money to the community and keeping people in town. You told me yourself. It's important to you and one of the reasons you came back home."

Sara questioned confiding in Jared. She'd let the comment slip one day when he asked her why she came home after law school. She didn't want to admit she came home because her mother pressured her. The comment made her look more like a homesick girl than the consummate professional she was.

Another reason not to confide in people, she thought.

"You still there, Sara?" Jared's voice broke into her thoughts.

"Yes. I'm here. Making some notes." She added, "Better to be prepared with Cynthia. I'll clear my calendar for tomorrow."

"Good. Also, prepare a response plan for the whole office. Everyone needs to be on the same page. I'd like to review it before it goes into effect. I'll be back at my desk at 7 a.m. Email it to me."

Wrinkling her nose, Sara glanced at the time. If she started working on it now, she might get home in time for four hours of sleep. Or she could sleep on the couch in the lobby and use her spare work clothes she kept in her office. She wondered what her partners would say when they learned she was using the office as her second home.

"You okay?" Jared asked. "Anything I can help with?"

Sara said, "No. It's under control. I'll have the plan to you in the morning."

Without waiting for his response, she hung up and turned

back to her computer screen. Now was the time to prepare for whatever Cynthia might say tomorrow. She needed a plan in place. Not to mention the fact, she planned to scrutinize the document Ron and Doug signed. No way was she letting either of them get away with destroying someone else's livelihood.

∼

THE LINE WENT dead in his hand. He held the phone out in front of him, wondering what exactly he managed to get involved in. Sara was competent. He knew that without a doubt. She'd made more progress on this project than any of his other local counsels ever had in the same amount of time. Her partners believed in her as well. She presented exactly like she was: a capable, intelligent professional. Not to mention an attractive and funny woman he found himself thinking about far too often.

The exact opposite of his assistant, whose termination today threw a wrench into his schedule. He should have done it months ago, but when he found out Monica neglected to pass on Seaton's last letter, he'd had enough. Monica could do her husband-shopping someplace else.

What was Seaton up to? The last letter he mailed out specifically stated Davis Investments was not a welcome addition, and yet the man was bold enough to approach Ron and Doug. Despite knowing Jared was 100% against his involvement. This was the first time the man had been bold enough to blatantly lie about something.

Something else bothered him. The connection between Doug and Davis Investment seemed too convenient. Leaning back in his chair, Jared closed his eyes as he considered how he got Doug's name. Maybe that was the connection. Someone had manipulated him into hiring Doug which inadvertently got Michael in the door.

He'd heeded Bill and Rich's advice about staying out of town, but this situation justified a trip to Glen Valley. Besides figuring out Michael's angle, the hiccup with the newspaper could get out of hand and added some urgency to a visit. And he hadn't seen Greg in action. This would give him time to meet some of the local businesses and smooth things over for Sara.

Shaking his head, he knew he was justifying the fact he wanted to see a woman, but he didn't care. He could use the trip to get to know Sara better on a personal level. She intrigued him with her self-sufficiency, but he was also curious about what kind of challenge she was up to. Her professional skills and abilities aside, he wanted to know if his gut was right. Was Sara Shaw the woman he'd been searching for?

"Shit. I sound like a bad romance novel," he grumbled. Tired of ruminating, Jared sat down at his computer to look for flights. With Monica out of the picture, he'd have to get used to doing things for himself until he found a replacement. The thought occurred to him he should find out if China wanted a job, but he tossed the idea aside. While it made sense according to the old adage *keep your friends close, and your enemies closer*, he felt like he owed something to Sara and her family. Had he dealt with Michael years ago, Sara wouldn't be in the middle of this now.

As soon as he got the flight scheduled, Jared pulled up the files he'd kept on Michael and his persistent requests. He scrolled through emails and contracts, most of which he'd never bothered to respond to. Jared wasn't sure what he was looking for, but it couldn't hurt to read through everything and have it fresh in his mind when he saw Sara. Something had to occur to him before he left. He'd look ridiculously pathetic if he showed up at Sara's with no plan on how to deal with Michael.

29

Sara parked her car in the newspaper's lot and turned off the ignition. A dull ache spread behind her eyes. The four hours of sleep she'd got the night before created a headache ibuprofen couldn't resolve. At least Jared approved her response plan. That was one thing she didn't have to worry about because she still had no idea what to do about Davis Investments.

She resisted resting her head on the steering wheel, in case someone walked by. Instead she closed her eyes and took several deep breaths. Maybe this wouldn't take long. Maybe she would go back to the office with a retraction in hand.

Opening her eyes, she dropped her head back against the headrest.

"Fat chance."

Realizing she couldn't put off the inevitable, Sara pulled her retraction request out of her briefcase and reread it. Everything looked good, but it had been late last night when she finished the letter, and everything needed to be in order. The quick review revealed it was as good as she remembered, and she relaxed.

"This is going to be fine," she said to herself. "A quick trip in and out, and I'll be back to the office."

Sara opened her car door and swung her legs out of the car. Before she stood up, she happened to glance down. She squinted, then blinked a few times as she looked at her shoes. A blue pump graced her left foot while her right foot sported a black one.

"No. I did not do this." She wiggled her feet and groaned. "This is what I get for buying the same shoes in different colors."

The sight reminded her of the time her sister came to her office wearing pig slippers. At the time, Sara thought it was ridiculous and only something her sister could manage. Boy, was she wrong.

Flexing her feet, Sara considered the situation. The shoes were both a dark color and complemented her navy pantsuit. At least, it wasn't more obvious.

"Maybe no one will notice."

She got out of her car, grabbed her purse, and headed to the office door. As she headed up the sidewalk to the door, it flung open. A man she didn't recognize stomped out. She kept her gaze forward as she continued up the path. When they passed each other, she heard him mumbling to himself, complaining about a missing sales flyer in his Sunday newspaper. Her optimism dropped. If the newspaper couldn't get a flyer right, how long would a retraction request take?

"Hey lady!"

She glanced back, realizing he was calling out for her. Putting her hand on the door, she said, "Yes?"

The man shrugged and pointed at her feet.

"Your shoes don't match. That's all." Without waiting for her response, the man whipped around and headed back to the parking lot.

Her shoulders drooped. As if this morning wasn't going to

be hard enough, she now had to deal with the fact her shoe mishap was more obvious than she thought. Shaking off her doubt, she quietly said, "I can do this."

Her patience took a hit when she saw a line of people waiting at the front desk. Taking her place in line, she craned her neck to see what the holdup was. From her place at the end of the line, she could see the one man behind the desk was multitasking. Not only was he handling the line of people, he was answering the phone, running the copy machine, and eating a bagel with a copious amount of cream cheese. His main priority appeared to be his bagel despite the fact the woman standing in front of him was yelling and the copy machine was angrily beeping.

"I want to know how my newspaper lands on my roof every morning." The woman stomped her foot before she continued. "The fire department won't come get it, and I can't reach it. But you still charge me for it, even though it isn't usable. What are you going to do about it?"

That makes one person who doesn't know about Cynthia's article, Sara thought. *Maybe no one got their newspapers today. Wouldn't that be great?*

Without uttering a sound, the man pulled a newspaper from the pile next to him and called something that sounded like "Next."

Damn. The newspaper's customer service is better than it looks.

The woman turned away from the reception desk and headed to the front door. Sara waited to hear what the person next in line wanted but before she could make out his request, the woman stopped next to her.

She squinted at Sara. "You're Helene's daughter, aren't you? The attorney?"

Knowing this was a loaded question, Sara put a pleasant expression on her face and nodded.

"Well then, you better get your footwear worked out before

your mother sees what you're wearing. I'm not sure if you know, but you have one blue shoe and one black shoe on." The woman's voice carried and everyone in line looked back at them. "My George used to do that all the time, rest his soul. He had an excuse, though. The dementia got him, yes it did. But you're young and healthy." Sara saw the woman's eyes get wider before she asked, "Did you do the walk of shame last night? Helene says her girls are above that so wouldn't this just be grand?"

Wishing she'd called instead of showing up in person, Sara ignored her warming cheeks and plastered a neutral expression on her face. "No ma'am. No walk of shame. I have the same pair in blue and black and accidentally grabbed one of each this morning."

The woman studied her, as if trying to decide if she was telling the truth. Sara didn't want to make a bigger scene than necessary, especially since she was here to fix another problem. She knew there would be fallout though. For all she knew, this woman played Bunco or cards with Helene.

"Hmmm. Well. I suppose." The woman shrugged then continued on her way.

When Sara looked toward the front of the line to see how things were going, she noticed everyone in front of her quickly looked away.

So much for keeping a low profile, she thought. The line moved up again and she relaxed a little. *Maybe this won't take much longer.*

Fifteen minutes later, Sara found herself the next person in line. She read through the retraction notice in her hand for the fifth time, looking for any typos, but she lost interest when she heard the man in front of her talking.

"Yes, my name is Thomas Radcliffe. I've got an appointment with Cynthia Anderson. She's expecting me."

Sara kept her eyes glued to her paper when she recognized

Thomas' name. She'd never returned the relationship coordinator's calls and had no interest in talking to him here in public. It did make her wonder why he was meeting with the reporter. But the bigger issue was she wouldn't be able to talk to Cynthia if the woman had an appointment. Why hadn't she called before she drove over?

"I'll let her know you're here," the man behind the counter said. He pointed toward some chairs in the corner. "You can wait over there."

"Thank you," said the man.

As he turned toward the sitting area, he paused. Sara saw his finger come into view as he pointed at her feet.

"Excuse me," Thomas said. "Did you know you're wearing two different colored shoes?"

Sighing in frustration, she nodded. "Yes. I grabbed the wrong pair of shoes. It was an accident. It was not a walk of shame. I was just in a hurry and grabbed the wrong damn shoes. Why is everyone so concerned about this?"

"A little grumpy this morning, Sara?" Cynthia interrupted her tirade. The reporter smiled as Sara saw her take in the situation. "I'm impressed. I expected the local counsel for The Miller Agency to call or email. Who knew I would rate a face-to-face visit?"

Before she could respond to Cynthia's taunting, Thomas said, "Sara? You're Sara Shaw?"

She reluctantly nodded, dreading what would come out of the man's mouth next.

"I'm Thomas Radcliffe, relationship coordinator." He extended his hand as he introduced himself. As she shook it, he continued. "I've been trying to get in touch with you. Your mother is very keen to find you a match."

Sara froze as she wondered if it was possible to spontaneously combust at will. Maybe she should've called the guy back. Because now, Cynthia had ammunition against her.

Tomorrow's headline, Sara thought. *Local attorney needs mommy's help to get a date.*

Resuming the handshake, Sara said, "Sorry Thomas. I have your message. Work has been busy lately."

"Your mother said you would be hard to reach. I'm a patient man though. It's what makes me good at my job."

"Well, thank you. If you don't mind, could I have a word with Cynthia before your meeting? It won't take long," said Sara.

Thomas nodded and pointed to the sofa. "I'll wait here. Ms. Anderson, you can come get me when you're ready." He settled himself on the sofa and pulled open a book with birds on the cover, as if this sort of thing happened to him all the time.

Sara steeled herself for the gloating look she expected to be on Cynthia's face, but she was surprised when she realized Cynthia looked tired rather than victorious.

"I'll be quick. You and I both know you never called me for a statement on your article."

Cynthia snarled at her.

"But I called your boss and he didn't respond."

Sara handed the retraction notice at the reporter. "Doesn't matter. Fix the problem. Get this announced today. Sign that last page agreeing to the terms, and I'll be out of your way so you and Thomas can meet."

The reporter grabbed the papers and read them. When she looked up after a minute, Cynthia waved the papers. "I'll make this happen. But I have to deal with Thomas first."

Curious, Sara tilted her head to the side. "Are you doing an article on dating services? Is that why he's here?"

As she studied the reporter's face, Sara recognized something. It was the look of a browbeaten daughter caught between a rock and a hard place. That's when Sara had her answer.

"Cynthia Anderson, you're his client, aren't you?"

The reporter's cheeks reddened, and she grabbed Sara's

arm, dragging her into an open conference room. Cynthia shut the door before she turned back to Sara and said, "I am. But you don't need to shout it all over the place."

Crossing her arms over her chest, Sara said, "As if you didn't think it was funny when Thomas outed me a minute ago."

"You're right. I did. But I'd appreciate it if you don't tell the entire town I'm desperate for a date."

Despite the fact that Cynthia wasn't her favorite person, Sara could empathize. But empathy only went so far. Business came first.

Pulling a pen from her briefcase, Sara said, "Sign this, and I'll get out of your way."

The reporter took the pen, twisting it between her fingers as she read the document. Rolling her eyes, Cynthia put the agreement on the table, signed it, and shoved it back at Sara.

"Happy now?"

"Ecstatic." Sara smoothed the paperwork and put it, and the pen, back in her briefcase. When she looked back up at Cynthia, she felt a pang of guilt. Cynthia clearly wasn't happy about Thomas being in the reception area. "Do you mind me asking why you need a date?"

Cynthia rolled her eyes.

"Of course, I mind, but you'll hear sooner or later. My mother wants to turn my bedroom into a pottery studio."

"That's old news."

"She said if I don't work with a dating coordinator, I have to move out of the house immediately."

Puzzled that Cynthia didn't see the obvious solution to the problem, Sara started to say this to Cynthia when she caught herself. Sara realized she was in the same predicament. Cynthia couldn't stand up to her mother and neither could Sara.

Instead, Sara said, "Well, good luck." Sara paused, before adding, "I actually really mean that. I know how manipulating mothers can be. No one deserves to be treated poorly. So, for what it's worth, I hope Thomas can help."

Pleased with what she considered a successful meeting, Sara nodded at Cynthia as she opened the door.

"I'll be on the lookout for the retraction."

"Thank you," said the reporter as she followed Sara out. "I guess it's time to meet my match."

Chuckling at the reporter's dry sense of humor, Sara headed out of the room to the main exit. She passed Thomas on her way out.

"So, I'll give you a call later today, Ms. Shaw and get on your schedule."

While the man's tenacity was impressive, Sara knew what she needed to do.

"No need, Thomas. Your services are unnecessary. Please feel free to tell my mother whatever you want, but I'll not be needing you."

Without waiting for his response, Sara walked out of the newspaper office and headed to her car. As she started the engine, she smiled.

"Now that wasn't such a bad start to the day after all!"

30

As soon as she stepped into the office, Sara groaned. People packed the lobby, most of them local business owners. Searching for Renee, she saw the receptionist hunched over her desk, her ear to the phone, scribbling frantically. Before she could make her way to her office, Sara heard someone say, "There she is," and a mass of irritated people surrounded her.

"How do I get my business on your radar?"

"Shame on you for not calling Cynthia back!"

"I'm a licensed electrician. You need those, don't ya?"

"Your mother is going to be so disappointed."

The comments bombarded her as Sara pushed through the mob toward Renee. The receptionist asked, "Can you hold please?" Without waiting for an answer, she jabbed the hold button and looked at Sara with wide eyes.

"It's been like this since I opened the doors. They either love you or hate you, but they're all loud about it! Whoever said no one reads the newspaper anymore was wrong. Flat out wrong! What did Cynthia say when you asked for a retraction?"

"She agreed. She'll get it out soon." Someone bumped into Sara, pushing her into the desk. "Okay, this isn't going to work."

"Sorry. I've been trying to keep everyone calm until you got here. What do you want to do?"

"I want to go work in my office, but we need to clear this place out," said Sara.

Renee frowned at her.

"That's brilliant! Why didn't I think of that?"

"You're in reactionary mode," Sara said, ignoring the woman's sarcastic tone. Looking around at the crowd, she added, "The stress of this group would do that."

"True. Speaking of stress, you've been getting some nasty phone calls. Joe said he's never giving you a membership at the gym."

"Seeing as I've never wanted one, I don't think that's going to be a problem. Okay. Time to get to work." Sara turned back to the people in the lobby. "Everyone. Please. Lower your voices and take a seat. I'd be happy to speak with each of you, but I can't hear you if you all talk at once."

The noise volume lowered a bit, and a small area cleared around Sara.

"Thank you. Now, I'm happy to meet with you, but let's do it with some semblance of order. Renee will pass around a piece of paper. Please write your name and number on it." Sara turned to Renee. "If anyone else comes in, have them sign in as well. Give me a couple of minutes, then you can send people back to my office."

Before she could even pass out the paper though, people began complaining.

"I was here first," someone called out.

Another voice shouted "I have an appointment in 30 minutes. I should go first."

A loud whistle pierced through the noise. Sara flinched at

the sound. The room fell silent after Renee let out another whistle.

"Enough! Now we're all adults here so let's start acting like it." She handed the person closest to her desk a clipboard and pen. "Put your names down and I'll put you in order. I remember who came in when." She held up a hand as a pudgy man wearing a bright orange hunting jacket came forward. "Yes, Mr. Hodges, I know you have to get back to your dogs. Put your name on the list and we'll get this moving."

Heading off toward her office, Sara felt someone tug at her elbow. She turned back to find Renee, a desperate look on her face.

"Would you consider driving over to Betty's? Free food does wonders to calm people's nerves. I'm thinking a few chocolate eclairs and blueberry scones might go a long way." Renee glanced at the clock. "If you leave now, you'll beat the lunch rush. Plus, you can take my car. It's parked out back and the keys are in it. You wouldn't have to wade through all these people again."

Before Sara could answer, the phone rang again, and Renee dashed back to her desk. Following the receptionist, Sara took the car keys from Renee's hand.

"Okay. I'll be back as soon as I can," Sara said low enough that none of the people in the lobby could hear. "And I'll bring you a raspberry Danish pastry for all the trouble!"

Renee flashed two fingers and mouthed "Hurry!"

Realizing she may not have a lot of time before the next wave of angry citizens arrived, Sara headed down the hall and out the back door.

∽

RENEE'S antique station wagon purred as Sara pulled into Betty's parking lot. She knew the receptionist did her own car maintenance, and she made a mental note to ask her if she wanted to start working on hers. In spite of the wood panel siding and decades old engine, the car ran perfectly.

"Clearly, I'm avoiding the reason I'm here," she said as she gave the steering wheel a pat. "Wish me luck."

She hopped out and noticed her mismatched shoes again.

"Damn it!" Wishing she had changed before she left her office, she shook her head and walked to the entrance of Betty's Coffee Bar. That's when she saw her mother's car parked next to the door. "Double damn it!"

Sara should have known Helene would be here. The Coffee Bar was the best place to catch up on gossip and her mother loved to hear what was happening. Cynthia's article brought enough people to the law firm, so why wouldn't it be a draw here?

Preparing herself for battle, Sara straightened her back and marched inside. Her mother leaned against the pastry case, a cup of coffee in her hand while Betty stood behind the display, boxing up food. Both women looked toward her when they heard her come in.

"We were just talking about you," said Helene with a smile. "Betty's putting goodies together for me. I planned to drop them by the office so I could hear all about my daughter, the one who doesn't return phone calls. At least I know now that it isn't just me you ignore."

Nodding slowly, Sara walked behind a display of gift cards and coffee mugs. Putting a physical barrier between her and her mother wouldn't solve the problem, but hopefully it would prevent her mother from seeing her mismatched shoes.

"Well, you know the media," Sara said. "Can't believe everything you read these days."

"I heard you have an office full of folks who do, though." Betty slid the box to Helene. "That will be $20 please." As her mother paid, Betty looked at Sara. "Speaking of which, Renee called ahead. She said you wanted some pastries to calm the angry masses back at your office. I'll get started on that. How about I get some raspberry Danish pastries wrapped up for Renee? I know she likes those." Betty grabbed an empty box from behind the counter. "I expect things will be back to normal in an hour or so."

"Thank you for helping, Betty. It is a zoo at the office and Renee said the phone has been ringing nonstop."

Helene's phone rang at that moment and she laughed.

"Guess it's contagious." She took the change Betty offered her and stepped toward the door. "Don't leave Sara. I've got to take this, but I want to talk to you."

Hoping she would be ready to leave before her mother got off the phone, Sara walked closer to the counter and patiently answered Betty's questions about who was waiting back at the law firm so that she could customize what pastries she sent back.

"Mr. Hodges only eats certain ones." Betty placed two Boston crème filled pastries in the box. "Those should mellow him out."

Sara smiled her thanks and took mental notes as Betty continued making recommendations on who liked what. By the time the woman closed the second box, Sara's head swam. She hoped people could figure out what they wanted on their own.

As she paid for the treats, she heard Helene return. Sara waited for her mother to speak, but Helene remained silent. Sara glanced up at Betty and saw Betty's eyes widen. Something was wrong.

Sara turned to assess the situation. Helene's expression reminded her of the time Blake presented his grandmother with a live spider for her birthday. She was horrified but faked a calm facade at the same time. Sara asked, "Is everything okay, Mom?"

"That was Thomas Radcliffe."

A shiver of annoyance went down Sara's spine. She didn't think Thomas would be so quick to report back to Helene. Taking a deep breath, Sara stood up straighter and asked, "And?"

"That's all you're going to say?" Helene asked. "You told Thomas Radcliffe you don't need his services and you didn't think to tell me?"

Sara shot a look at Betty, but Betty took a step away from the counter. Betty might be willing to help her with the locals, but Sara knew she was on her own with her mother. Steeling herself for her mother's reaction, Sara said, "When I'm ready to date, I'll figure it out on my own."

Helene's nostrils flared, but she remained silent. Recognizing an impending temper tantrum, Sara waited for whatever came next. She didn't have to wait long when she noticed Helene staring at her shoes.

"You can't even put on matching shoes. How are you going to get a date?"

The ridiculous question unsettled Sara more than her mother's anger. Sara glanced at Betty, but the coffee shop owner had bent down behind the counter. The idea that Betty was using the display as a shield from Helene's anger was comical.

Hearing the jingle of car keys, Sara looked back at her mother, who retreated out of the store. A sinking feeling in Sara's stomach made her wonder if she'd pushed her mother too far. Before she could ask Betty's opinion, she saw the pastry box on the counter. Sara grabbed it and followed her mother outside.

"Mom, wait! You left this," Sara called after her mother, holding out the box.

Helene paused after she opened her car door.

"I bought them for you. Take them to the office or throw them away. I don't care." Sara swore she saw a single tear fall down Helene's face before her mother brushed it away. She opened her car door but paused. "You know, I only wanted to help. It's clear to me why you haven't found anyone special yet. Anyone as hard-hearted as you isn't easy to love."

Without waiting for a response, Helene slid into her car and slammed the door. Sara stood, watching Helene drive out of the lot. She stayed there until she felt Betty standing next to her.

"She didn't mean that. Your mother's just mad that she didn't get to rescue you."

Confused and slightly hurt by her mother's reaction, Sara nodded.

"I guess," she said. Sara sighed. "To think I came over here for some good treats and I ended up with that."

Giving her a sympathetic smile, Betty handed Sara the boxes of pastries.

"Shake it off. She'll get over it. Right now, you need to focus on that silly newspaper article. Then you can deal with Helene."

Knowing she didn't have a choice; Sara loaded the boxes into Renee's station wagon. All she could do now was head back to the office and focus on what she could control. And Helene was definitely wasn't it.

31

Sara used the back entrance of the office, avoiding the angry mob in the lobby. She made it to her office the same time as Renee. Thrusting the boxes of pastries into Renee's hands, she said "Here. The raspberry ones are in the smaller box. Use the others as a peace offering."

Renee peeked inside of the box and grinned.

"Betty rocks."

Putting her purse and briefcase down, Sara flipped on her computer as she shook her head.

"Not just Betty. My mother planned to drop off some pastries, too." The computer beeped several times as it warmed up. "Only she left a little angry with me. She's not a happy camper."

"Not much of a news flash there."

Interesting how Renee considers my mom's reaction normal, thought Sara while she pulled out her chair and sat down. She adjusted the pen and notepad that sat on the right side of her desk. When Renee started to speak, Sara waved her away. "I don't want to talk about it."

Pursing her lips, Renee shrugged.

"Okay. Well, I'm going to console the crowd with sugar. Let me know what else you need from me."

Renee closed the door, and Sara let out a sigh. She knew that Helene was upset and trying to irritate her, but she hated how much it affected her. Renee didn't deserve to be shooed away, but Sara couldn't stand to talk about it.

Luckily, her inbox popped up on the screen. Sara stared at the 128 new messages, several boasting urgent flags. Good thing she and Cynthia were on the same page because she didn't think she could make it through all these complaints on her own. Scrolling through the messages, she felt sure the retraction would take care of most of them. As soon as the newspaper's website posted the correction, she would craft an email and send it out to everyone. That took care of one problem.

But it didn't take care of Helene. She tapped her fingers on her desk, debating what she should do. If Helene was that upset, she was liable to shoot her mouth off with anyone she met. That could cause another backlash. The best defense was a good offense, at least that was what made the most sense right now.

Sara grabbed her phone and punched in her father's cell number. She stood up from her desk, bent over at the waist and touched her toes as she waited for a response. Her quads screamed in opposition. Shaking her head, she promised herself to make it to yoga again tonight, regardless of what happened during the day.

"Well hello honey. I was expecting your call." Max chuckled. "Whatever you did to your mother, it sent her into a tizzy."

Standing up, she glanced at the clock.

"How did she get home that fast?"

"She's not home. She called from the car."

"Whoa. She's really mad." Everyone knew Helene was opposed to using her cell phone when driving. If she called Max from the road, Sara knew Helene would be out of sorts for days. Maybe weeks. "She walked out on me at Betty's. I figured she wanted me to follow her and beg for forgiveness, but I don't have time for that today. The office is full of disgruntled community members."

"There is nothing you can do, Sara. Let her be."

His words surprised her. As she let the words sink in, she realized how uncomfortable it made her.

"I don't want her mad at me. We both know that's a recipe for disaster." Sara walked to the window and stared out. Several cars were pulling out of the parking lot. Renee must have calmed people down enough. Or maybe it was the sugar in the Danish pastries. Either way, they were going home. "Really, Dad. What should I do?"

When Max didn't immediately answer, Sara felt her pulse quicken.

"Come on. You always have an idea how to fix things."

"Sara, why do you want to fix this?"

"Because she's my mother and I'm supposed to," said Sara with a sigh. "Respect your elders or something like that."

"Does she respect you?"

The question startled her.

"Well. No. She doesn't. She treats me like I'm a child." Sara thought about it and added, "She's treating me like she used to treat Tasha. At least before Tasha and Greg got together."

"Exactly. Now she's my wife and I love her dearly, but the two of you have to figure this out on your own."

"She asked you what to do, didn't she?" It dawned on Sara that her mother called her father for advice as well. "Did you tell her the same thing?"

She heard the laugh in his voice when he answered.

"Yes, and her response was oddly similar to yours. The two of you need a break from each other. Go live your life. Once she realizes you're fine without her approval, she'll back off. That's what she did with Tasha."

"Why are you telling me this now?" Sara sat on the corner of her desk. "This would have been beneficial info to have a few years ago."

"Kiddo, I can only tell you so much. One of you is going to have to take the initiative, and you and I both know who it's going to be. You are an incredibly smart woman, but you and Tasha don't always think things through when it comes to your mother. Stop trying to be something you're not and do what you want. Forget about us. We'll be fine. But I need you to be okay." She heard a door slam and her mother's voice call out. "Gotta go. I love you. Your mother loves you too, in her own way. I know you'll figure this out."

Unsettled by her father's advice, Sara slid off the desk and walked to her chair. Max never got involved with his wife's schemes and conflicts. She knew he didn't condone them, but he'd always said that people have to make up their own minds about important issues in life. If she was to infer anything from the conversation, then she should screw her head back on, ignore her mother, and get to work.

The problem was she couldn't ignore the fact that her mother was unhappy, which made everyone around her unhappy. If Helene held a grudge against you, you'd know it. Sara felt guilty, remembering the look her mother had given Betty at the coffee shop. Betty didn't deserve to be on the receiving end of Helene's shenanigans. Sara owed Betty too much to leave her at the mercy of her mother.

"What's the solution?" she muttered to herself.

Her computer dinged, interrupting her introspection. The newspaper's retraction sat in her inbox.

At least something is going my way, thought Sara.

Taking a deep breath, she tilted her head from side to side, stretching her neck. Then, she shrugged her shoulders to her ears, then dropped them down where they belonged as she exhaled. She didn't know if it was the stress of the newspaper or

Helene, but Sara's entire body felt tight and on alert. Fighting to relax, she closed her eyes and took deep breaths to calm herself.

In spite of her efforts, her father's words echoed in her head. "There's nothing you can do. Let her be." Maybe Max was right. She ought to let go of her irritation with Helene and focus on the task at hand. She pushed aside any more thoughts about her mother. She had work to do.

32

Sara craned her head, looking out the window toward the parking lot. The sun reflected off the one car still left there. The newspaper retraction worked. Or maybe it was the pastries. Quite honestly, Sara didn't care so long as everything settled down.

She turned back to Greg's email. The newspaper article spurred a few people to show up on at the riverfront to protest the renovation of the buildings. So far, they were being reasonable and only wanted to have their opinions heard. Greg promised a long list of opinions in his next email.

He'd also had a plethora of tradespeople drop in to find out if The Miller Agency was hiring. The project no longer had a shortage of welders and plumbers. Happy that the article did something positive, Sara turned her attention to the agreement Ron and Doug signed with Michael when her phone rang.

Wondering if there was a residual issue from the newspaper retraction, Sara answered. "What's up Renee?"

"Your 3 p.m. is here. Do you want to set up in your office or the conference room?"

Glancing at her calendar, Sara didn't see an appointment.

She frowned. Helene was too mad to show up again today. Her niece and nephew would be getting home from school soon, so Tasha wouldn't be here. The only other person that made sense was Jared. But he didn't get in until tomorrow so they could discuss what to do about Michael.

"I don't have anything scheduled. Who is it?"

"Thomas Radcliffe. I didn't have it down either, but he said you ran into him at the newspaper office this morning. Something about doing a favor for Cynthia." Renee's voice dropped to a whisper. "For a relationship coordinator, this guy seems a little weird. All he's been talking about since he arrived is some bird he saw when he drove in. I'd peg him as an ornithologist, not a dating specialist."

Sara pinched the bridge of her nose. She'd been clear that she was not going to be his client. There was no ambiguity in what she said or meant. Sighing, she started to ask Renee to dispatch him, but changed her mind.

"Send him to the conference room. I'll be there in a second."

She activated her screen saver, grabbed her pen and notepad and headed out of her office, narrowly missing Rich as she dashed toward the conference room.

"Hey, what's the rush? Are you really that excited to get a date?" Rich smirked at her when she stopped in her tracks and glared at him. "That is the relationship coordinator, isn't it? I heard he's been calling." Tilting his head toward the conference room, he asked, "Can I meet him?"

"No."

Rolling her eyes, she continued on her way, stopping at the door of the room to observe Thomas. He stared out the window, making an odd noise. Before she could ask what he was doing, a bird landed on the branch outside the window. Thomas drew circles on the window with his finger. The bird followed the movement and made a similar noise back to him.

Not wanting to startle him, Sara softly rapped on the door. He turned, his cheeks red and his eyes twinkling.

"Did you know there is a crimson-bellied conure outside? Someone must have let it loose. Or maybe it escaped. I thought I saw it on the way in... but look!" Thomas pointed at the bird with excitement. "She's right there. Amazing. If she's still there when we're finished, do you mind if I try to catch her? I can't imagine she'll last long in the wild."

Questioning whether the town could be classified as wild, Sara nodded.

"Sure. She's all yours."

A huge smile covered Thomas face. "I know it seems strange. A relationship coordinator excited about a bird. But everyone has to have a hobby."

Sara didn't know what to say to that, so she gestured to the table.

"Please take a seat."

Thomas glanced longingly back at the window.

"If it's okay with you, I'm going to stand. I want to keep an eye on her. Just in case."

"Suit yourself," said Sara as she pulled out a chair and sat down. She wanted to make this a quick conversation. "Mr. Radcliffe—"

"Please, call me Thomas."

Frowning, Sara continued. "Okay. Thomas. What are you doing here? I made it clear at the newspaper office I'm not interested in working with you."

"Oh, I know. But the problem is your mother prepaid for the services." Thomas never took his eyes off the bird.

"Refund her money. That seems pretty simple."

"I wish it were. But your mother signed up for The Works, and you can't just cancel that."

The thought crossed her mind that she was being recorded for some practical joke show. She glanced around the room looking for cameras as she said, "That sounds like a type of hotdog. Or a car wash."

Nodding, Thomas agreed. "I hear that a lot. I've suggested to management we change the name, but that's what I have to work with for now." He looked wistfully out the window before he turned back to her. "But your mother paid for the package, so I have to fulfill the services."

"There's no cancellation clause?"

Pulling a document out of his bag, he handed it to her.

"This is our standard contract. Feel free to review it for yourself, but you'll see it's nonrefundable."

Sara took a moment to skim through. Thomas was correct. Her mother agreed to a no-termination clause as well as a no-refund clause. She doubted Helene bothered to read the contract. But her mother did this without her permission, and Sara wasn't going to feel guilty about not using it.

"Do you often have parents hiring you for their children?"

Thomas flushed. "I'm not at liberty to give specifics. Confidentiality, you know."

Sara struggled to hold in a laugh. Somehow, she didn't think relationship counselor-client privilege existed.

"Yes, but what about an estimate? No names needed."

"Well, I suppose that wouldn't hurt." Thomas waved to the bird and walked to the table. "I've seen a sharp uptick in mothers contacting me about their daughters. Not so much sons. I probably have a hundred inquiries a month. Maybe half of those register with me."

"What is the cost for The Works?" Sara couldn't help herself. "What am I leaving on the table?"

The man hesitated. "Technically, I'm not at liberty to discuss pricing, but since your mother already paid, I suppose it's okay. Usually, it's $5,000."

Sara stifled her gasp. "You say usually. What did my mother pay?"

"She got in on a special we were running. Buy one, get one free."

"So, she split it with someone," Sara said more to herself than to Thomas. She wondered if Cynthia got her services on special as well. Gesturing down at the papers, she asked, "Provided I don't find a way out to get my mother's money back—"

"You won't," Thomas said.

"Can I gift the services to someone?"

"N—" Thomas cut himself off before finishing the word. "Well, I don't know. No one has asked before. I don't see why not, but I'd have to review the contract to see."

"You do that and get back to me. I may have an idea of someone who would enjoy this." Renee complained about a lack of suitable dating material. Despite her flaws, the receptionist deserved a chance to find someone special. Sara hoped Renee agreed, or she'd be back to square one. Standing up, Sara extended her hand. "It was nice to talk with you."

Taking her hand, Thomas said, "And you. I have to say you're much more pleasant than your mother made you out to be."

Sara stopped mid-handshake. Leave it to Helene to get a dig in even when she wasn't around. As she tried to drop his hand, Thomas tightened his hold and placed his other hand on top.

"I'm sorry. I didn't mean for that to come out like that. But Ms. Shaw, I've seen a lot of things in my line of work. Your mother is not unique, though she is extreme. Don't let her stop you from doing your own thing." He gestured around the room. "You have a lot going for you. It would be a shame if you let her derail it."

The bird rapped again at the window, and Sara saw the excitement return to Thomas' eyes. A tinge of regret hit Sara. She didn't have anything that made her look like that.

"I think she's waiting for you."

"She is." Thomas grabbed his satchel as he headed toward

the door. As he left, he said "If you ever change your mind, give me a call. I could find you someone special."

She nodded and waited until she heard him say goodbye to Renee. There was no reason to tell him she might have already found her own someone special.

33

"You did what?" Helene cringed at the sound of her husband's voice. She couldn't remember the last time he'd raised his voice. "What were you thinking? You've outdone yourself this time, Helene."

Irritation flooded through her as she realized Max didn't take her side. How was it her fault that Sara was offended by her offer to help? Part of her responsibility as a mother was to guide her children and that was all she was doing by hiring the relationship coordinator.

She closed her eyes to Max's pacing, and the image of the coffee shop played on her internal movie screen. Betty hiding behind the counter while Sara explained what was happening. "My actions were fine. And for heaven's sake, I only complained about her mis-matched shoes once. Can you believe it? She was wearing one black and one blue one?"

Her eyes shot open at the guttural sound that filled the room. Max's half scream, half groan sent shivers down her spine and told her just how far she'd pushed her husband.

"Who the hell cares what color her shoes were? Don't change the subject. This is our family. Our daughter, in case you haven't noticed, who has been working her ass off for the last three months."

"Of course, I'm aware of the situation. She's been busy with the new job. I've dropped by a few times to see if I can help—"

"You badger her." Max held up his hand. "At least have the decency to call a spade a spade."

Helene crossed her arms across her chest. "That's a bit harsh, don't you think? I'm her mother. I'm supposed to be firm."

"What a crock of shit."

Her eyes widened. Max rarely cursed.

He's losing his patience, thought Helene. *And this isn't even all my fault. Sara overreacted as well.*

"There's no reason for that kind of language. Plus, this show of temper isn't good for your blood pressure. You know what Dr. Howell said."

"To hell with what he said. You probably told him what to say so you could dictate my life, too."

Helene's own heart rate picked up. She and Max fought now and then. Any married couple did. But this was outside the norm. Picking a speck of lint off of her silk shirt, she lamented this conversation hadn't gone the way she wanted. Nothing she said now was going to change Max's mind about the situation, so it was best to move onto something else.

"Have you heard from Tasha? I'm wondering when that Greg boy is going to pop the question?"

The silence that greeted Helene's question made her think Max had left the room. She turned around expecting to see an empty kitchen. Instead, her husband shook his head and glared at her.

"Have we not been in the same conversation? At what point do you think it's a good idea to poke your nose in our daughters' business? Both of our daughters." She opened her mouth to speak, but he cut her off. "No more. I know you think you're doing this for the best interest of our girls, but it's not. You owe Sara an apology."

"Well, she needs to apologize to me."

Her husband shook his head and grabbed his keys from the counter. "I'm going to the bowling alley. Don't worry about me for dinner."

"Wait!" Helene called out, but the side door slammed shut. "Well. How rude."

She took several breaths to steady herself. Helene debated following Max, but that was demeaning. No, she would go ahead with her plans for the evening and let Max come to his senses.

Tonight was Bunco. Sara flustered her so much she'd forgotten to pick up her dessert tray from Betty's this morning. Irritated that Betty hadn't called to remind her, she grabbed her phone and punched in Betty's number.

"Betty's Coffee Bar."

"It's me, Betty."

"I know. What can I do for you?"

Tamping down her irritation that Betty wasn't going to be as helpful as she hoped, Helene smoothed down her hair. "When I left this morning, I was in a rush and forgot to get my order for Bunco tonight. I was wondering if you could bring it with you when you come."

"No can do. I've got dinner with the grandkids. Family before friends, you know. I'm here for another hour or so. You'll have to come pick up the tray on your way." Someone shouted in the background and Betty paused. "Yeah, it's Helene. She forgot the dessert tray." Helene strained to hear the conversation, but she couldn't make out what was being said.

"Who is that?"

"You're in luck. That was Cybil Anderson. She's here for the sandwich tray. She'll take the desserts, too, so you don't have to make another trip. How's that?"

The thought of the schoolteacher arriving with her petit fours nauseated her, but unless she wanted to make an extra trip, she'd have to take what she could get. Helene would arrive early though, to make sure everyone knew the desserts were from her and not Cybil.

"That's fine. Tell her thank you for me."

"Tell her yourself," Betty barked, then asked, "How do you plan to pay?"

Taken aback by Betty's harsh tone, Helene said, "I'll come by tomorrow and settle up."

"Hmmm. Make it after the coffee rush. I don't want a bunch of customers put off by your behavior. Today was bad enough."

Insulted by Betty's remark, Helene started to complain, but she realized Betty had already hung up. She stared at the phone in her hand. What had gotten into everyone today? First, Sara, then Max. Now Betty. They were acting like *she'd done* something wrong.

Shaking off the confusion, she headed to her room. She needed to hurry if she wanted to beat Cybil to Bunco. As she pulled her lucky sweater set out of the drawer, she calculated she had time to stop by Tasha's. Maybe her younger daughter could give her some insight as to why everyone was irritated. Plus, she could find out if Tasha was engaged yet. Helene had some spectacular ideas for the wedding.

34

"Cereal bowl goes in the dishwasher, Blake. Not the sink. We've talked about that before."

Her son trudged back into the kitchen.

"But you're standing there. Why don't you put it in?"

"Because I didn't put it there in the first place. Do it right the first time so you don't have to redo it." She watched as he put the bowl and spoon into the dishwasher, then turned and walked away. She cleared her throat.

"What did I do now?" Blake asked with his arms crossed in front of him.

Tasha hid her grin as she watched her little boy prepare to deny any wrongdoing. *Check that,* she thought. *He's not really little anymore.*

"Close the dishwasher."

Blake frowned.

"Mom, when I grow up, I'm gonna use paper plates so all I have 'ta do is throw 'em away. None of this dishwasher business."

Nodding, Tasha asked, "What about the environment? I

thought you and Libby agreed that you needed to downsize your carbon footprint to help the earth heal itself."

"What do paper plates have to do with that?"

"Less trash in the landfill." Tasha pointed at the sink. "We already have plates and cups so there isn't any waste."

"We'd be better off not eating meat and riding our bikes to school, Mom." Libby walked up behind her brother. "Statistics show that paper's carbon footprint is minimal. We have to take bigger action if we're going to save the planet."

Rather than get into a debate with her daughter, Tasha switched topics.

"Aunt Sara is babysitting this weekend. Do you know what you want to do?"

Before either of the kids answered, the phone rang. Libby dashed to the counter and picked it up before Tasha could react.

"Hello?"

Tasha waited patiently for Libby to find out who was on the phone. Nine times out of ten, it was a sales call, but occasionally, someone wanted to talk to her.

"May I ask who is calling please?" Libby glanced at her mother then put her hand over the mouthpiece of the phone.

"She says it's Cynthia Anderson from *The Gazette*. I thought Mrs. Anderson was Blake's teacher."

Reaching out for the phone, Tasha put her hand over the receiver. "Cynthia is Blake's teacher's daughter. Did she say what she wanted?"

"Something about Aunt Sara's date."

Before she could ask further questions, Libby skipped out of the kitchen with Blake following quickly behind. Scowling at her son's back, she closed the door to the dishwasher.

"Hello?"

"Tasha, this is Cynthia Anderson, over at *The Gazette*. How are you today?"

"Fine." Knowing the trouble Cynthia caused her sister, Tasha grabbed her cell phone and pulled up her recording app. Tasha refused to get caught in the middle of whatever the reporter was up to now. "Just so you know, I'm recording this conversation."

"Fair enough. After what happened with your Sara, I can understand. Let me get to the point. What do you know about Michael Seaton and Davis Investments?"

Immediately on alert, Tasha said, "Only what I read in your article. Something about an investment in the project on the riverfront."

"Mr. Seaton said he knows your husband. Doug invested in several of Mr. Seaton's projects. Can you confirm?"

Feeling feisty, Tasha said, "I don't have a husband. I can confirm that."

"Oh, you know what I mean. Do you know what's going on?"

"I don't. You'll have to talk with Doug if you want more information." Finished with the conversation, Tasha asked, "Do you need anything else? I'd like to get back to the kids."

The reporter paused, and Tasha scrunched up her face. She should've stopped while she was ahead. Of course, the woman needed something. She needed a story or a lead or some gossip to write about. Tasha knew better than to offer up information to someone in the media.

"What do you know about Thomas Radcliffe?"

Grinning, Tasha said,

"Sorry. Can't help you there either. Have a good evening."

"Wait—"

Tasha hung up the phone before Cynthia could ask her anything else. She stopped the recording on her phone and texted it to her sister with a note.

Just talked to Cynthia. Here is the recording. What's going on?

After sending the text, the doorbell rang. She waited a few

seconds, to see if the kids would answer it, but the chime sounded again. Leaving her cell phone on the counter, Tasha headed to the living room. She peaked through the window and saw her mother's car sitting in the driveway.

Rolling her eyes, she took a deep breath before answering the door.

"Hi Mom. How are you today?"

Helene grabbed her left hand. She squeezed it once, then dropped it and glided to the sofa. By the time Tasha realized her mother was checking for an engagement ring, Helene was seated gracefully on the couch, touching up her lipstick.

"Fine. Just thought I'd stop by before Bunco."

Tasha heard her phone sound.

"I've got to get that. Do you want anything from the kitchen? A water?"

Helene pulled the sides of her sweater together. "No, thank you. I only have a minute. Your phone can wait."

"Actually, it can't. I'll be right back."

Without waiting for her mother's response, Tasha walked to the kitchen and checked her phone. The text from Sara rang again.

Don't tell C anything. Will call later.

"*If you listened to my message, you know I didn't,*" Tasha mumbled to herself before texting back.

What about Mom? She's sitting on my couch.

On your own there was Sara's immediate reply.

"I bet they had a fight. That explains why she's sitting my couch." Determined not to get involved, Tasha headed back into the living room, where Libby had joined her grandmother. Tasha watched from the door, listening to see what information Helene would try to pump from her granddaughter.

"School's good, Grandma. I like it a lot."

"Do you see Mrs. Anderson much?" Tasha perked up when she heard her mother asking about Blake's teacher. Why would

Helene care what the teacher was doing? Something was suspicious, especially considering Tasha just got off the phone with Mrs. Anderson's daughter. Coincidences usually meant something was up, especially where her mother was concerned. "Tell me, Libby. What do you think of her?"

Before Libby could answer, Tasha stepped back into the room.

"I'm back. Libby, your grandma has to get going. She has Bunco tonight."

"I have a few minutes," Helene protested.

Libby leaned in to give her grandmother a hug. "That's okay. I have homework. Good luck tonight!" Libby waved as she skipped out of the room.

Tasha waved back then turned to Helene. Her mother's eyes followed Libby, letting her assess her mother. She was impeccably dressed as usual, but Helene fidgeted with her purse. Her make-up looked a little brighter than usual, as if she'd applied extra to compensate for something.

Not just a fight. An argument! Tasha thought.

"Are you okay?" she asked her mother.

Tasha swore Helene's face darkened. She didn't know if her mother was blushing or if she was wearing too much bronzer. Either way, Helene was off her game.

"Of course. I'm fine. Like I said, I had a minute before Bunco and thought I'd stop by." She stood, smoothing down her perfectly pressed pants and headed for the door. "I'll just go then. I don't want to be late."

Chuckling to herself, Tasha wondered if she should mention the fight with Sara. Since she didn't have all the details, she thought better of it. Instead she had a better idea. "You could've just called to see if Greg proposed."

Her mother's face froze, reminding her of the look on Blake's face when he flushed Libby's diary down the toilet.

"I don't know what you're talking about, young lady." When

Helene waved away the accusation, Tasha knew she was right. It wasn't nice, but it felt good to have the advantage over her mother for once. Rather than press her luck, Tasha walked to the door and opened it for Helene.

"Whatever you say. Enjoy tonight."

Her mother patted her hair before taking her keys from her purse.

"I'll try. Apparently, Cybil Anderson is bringing sandwiches as her contribution. I hope she skips the onions. It's rude to give everyone bad breath." Tasha thought for a second Helene was going to say something else, but instead she leaned in for a quick hug, before turning and walking to her car.

Tasha watched her mother drive off. Her mother never ceased to amaze her. Always snooping. Except tonight, Helene was caught red-handed.

"Score one for me," Tasha said as she closed the door and went in search of her kiddos.

35

"So, what's this I read about Michael Seaton and Davis Investments?" Bill walked into Sara's office unannounced and settled himself into a side chair. Glancing up from her computer, she watched her partner fold his hands across his midsection and waited for her response.

Irritated that Bill felt he could badger her for information about The Miller Agency's business, she returned her attention to the email she was typing. She finished it and pressed "send" before turning to Bill. "I don't know. What did you read?"

Bill's eyebrows shot up, and she knew she'd hit a nerve. He didn't like it when she pushed back, but after everything she'd dealt with yesterday, Sara was tired of people questioning her capabilities.

"People swarmed our lobby complaining about how the renovation isn't good for the town. It reflects poorly on our firm when one of our own doesn't behave in a civilized and professional manner."

Anger had her sitting forward. To give herself time to calm down, Sara propped her chin on her hands and counted to five before she spoke.

"I'm aware of the situation as I handled it. The newspaper made an error and has since retracted it. The retraction clearly states that I was never contacted and there is no financial relationship between The Miller Agency and Davis Investments. Cynthia lied, as did Doug and Ron." She knew her next comment would deliberately provoke Bill, but she couldn't help herself. "I believe you partook in some of the damage control. How were those two blueberry scones?"

Popping out of his seat, Bill said, "You don't have to be rude about it. I'm pointing out that your actions impact all of us here at the law firm."

Knowing he would never agree that some of his own actions were inappropriate as well, Sara sat quietly and waited to see what happened next. She was finished being micromanaged by her partners.

"What did Jared say when you told him about it?"

Sighing, she pushed away from her desk and stood up. Bill would never accept that she was capable of making decisions on her own for her own clients. Rather than attempt to explain his lack of faith in her, she simply said, "We're going to talk about it when he gets here." Sara looked at her watch. "I'm expecting him later this afternoon."

"You could've told him over the phone. He didn't need to fly into town just so you could explain a few misunderstandings to him." Bill tapped Sara's desk. "Why is he really coming for another visit?"

Now that's none of your business, thought Sara despite the fact she didn't know the answer. It did, however, fit in well with her plans. After yesterday's debacle with her mother and the lack of respect from her partners, she'd decided. It was time to make a move. She didn't want to share her decision with Bill until she talked to Jared, so she just shrugged. "He said he had some things he wants to discuss in person."

Bill put his hands in his pockets and walked to the door.

"Give me a call when he gets here. I'd like to say hello. And remind him what a great job you're doing."

From that conversation, I wouldn't have gathered my performance was great, she thought. *And why not just compliment me directly.*

Sara relaxed when her partner left. She didn't know how long she'd felt this constant antagonism around Bill and Rich, but it was confirmation. Her time at the law firm needed to end.

The phone rang. Grateful for the distraction, Sara answered it.

"You said you were calling later. I thought that meant the same day," Tasha said. "Way to leave me hanging."

Sara smiled at the sound of her sister's voice.

"Well, you're always welcome to call me. Clearly, you have my number."

"Touché. But it's more fun to give you a hard time about it. So, what exactly is going on?"

As quickly as she could, Sara explained how Ron and Doug signed an unauthorized investment agreement with Davis Investments.

"Sounds like something Doug would do. I'm surprised Ron helped him, but people do strange things. Speaking of strange, why would Cynthia lie about calling you?"

"Her excuse was she called Jared. I work for Jared. Ergo, she called me."

"Geez, even I know better than that," said Tasha. "Now that that's resolved, tell me what's going on with you and Mom. She made a surprise visit yesterday afternoon and asked Libby about Mrs. Anderson."

Sara took a deep breath before she answered.

"We had a fight."

"Ya think?"

"No, this was the fight to end all fights." Sara prepared herself to tell Tasha her decision. "I'm not doing this anymore."

"Doing what? Listening to Mom make stupid remarks?"

Standing up, Sara squared her shoulders. She was more than ready to stand up for herself but considering all the grief she'd given her sister over the years, Sara was nervous.

"You still there?" her sister asked when she didn't answer immediately.

"Yes," said Sara. Walked across her office and closed the door. She didn't need anyone else hearing this before she was ready. "I'm finished with letting Mom make things difficult for me. Actually, I'm tired of dealing with Rich and Bill's behavior, too."

When Tasha didn't respond, Sara jokingly echoed her sister's earlier question, "You still there?"

Tasha cleared her throat. "I am. I'm just a little concerned about where this is going."

"As soon as this project is over, I'm looking for a new law firm." Sara bent forward into swan dive.

"Your voice got muffled." Tasha asked, "Are you doing yoga while we talk?"

Sara smiled as she rose to mountain pose. "Yes, I am. I've been neglecting myself for a while, but I'm getting back on track." Sliding her foot up the inside of her leg, she rooted herself in Tree Pose before continuing. "I don't know what Jared is going to say—"

"Why don't you ask for a transfer to Chicago? Jared would be stupid not to take you on."

"You might be biased."

"Of course, I am. I'm your sister."

"Regardless of whether Jared wants me or not, it's time for me to get out of here." Sara adjusted her stance to keep her balance and said, "I stayed too long. Honestly, I never should've come back after law school."

"I'm glad you did, though."

"There were a few good things that resulted from coming home," said Sara as she lost her balance and put both feet on the ground. "Take us for instance. If I hadn't come back, you and I wouldn't be such good friends, now would we?"

"True." Tasha asked, "Who's going to finish the project?"

"It might take me some time to find what I want, so I'll be around for a while. Besides, Greg is more than capable. Even if I do find something immediately, I can make visits back to town."

"Will you come back for a wedding?"

"Sure, I will." Sara stopped as sister's words clicked. She smiled in excitement. "Wait a minute. Did Greg propose?"

"I wanted to tell you in person, but this will have to work. He surprised me last night with the ring. Funny timing, too, because when Mom came over yesterday afternoon, she checked out my ring finger, like she expected to find something there." Sara considered telling her sister that Greg shared his plans with Max and Helene, but she didn't have to. "Greg told me he asked Dad for his permission, but he seemed surprised Mom gave things away."

"Did she really give them away, though?" Sara sat down on the floor butterfly style and bent forward to stretch her back.

"No, she didn't. It makes me happy that Greg was comfortable enough to talk to Dad, but Mom is what she is. I doubt she'll ever change." Tasha paused before she continued, "But, Sara, I think this is a good move for you. I'll miss you, but you need to be someplace else. Getting some distance between you and Mom will be good. Just promise to be at the wedding."

"That I can promise." Popping up from the floor, Sara looked at her clock. "Okay, I need to finish up a few things so I'm ready for Jared."

"K. Well, good luck. Text me and let me know what he says. And Sara?"

"Yes?"
"I'm really happy for you!"
Sara swallowed back the tears that threatened.
"I'm happy for you, too!"

36

When Jared walked into the law office, he was pleasantly surprised to find a calm lobby and quiet background music. The receptionist behind the desk wasn't familiar, but China was here the last time he was in town. So were Sara's niece and nephew, come to think of it. As he recalled the chaos of that day, he decided he preferred this rendition of the office over the other.

"Penny for your thoughts," said the woman behind the desk.

Her informality surprised him, but he played along.

"Just thinking this visit is starting out much better than my last time."

"That would be partially my fault." She stood up, walked around the desk, and put out her hand. "I'm Renee, the regular receptionist. You must be Mr. Hughes. It's a pleasure to meet you. Ms. Shaw is expecting you. Can I get you some coffee?"

Shaking her hand, he said, "No, but I could use a bottle of water."

"Sure. Feel free to take a seat, and I'll be right back."

Jared circled around the room, examining the pictures on

the wall. He'd been too distracted last time. The room had a professional but comfortable feel about it that he'd missed the first time around.

A watercolor of a beach caught his attention, and he stopped to admire it. It reminded him of a vacation he took too long ago. Maybe when this project was finished, he'd take a trip someplace warm with sand and tropical drinks.

I wonder if Sara is the piña colada type or if she's more into daiquiris?

Closing his eyes, he shook his head to banish the thought from his mind. He didn't know what was getting into him lately. This was a business trip. Only a business trip.

"Here's your water," Renee said, bringing him back to reality. "Let me show you to the conference room."

Jared followed Renee, though he remembered the way from his last trip. When they got to the room, Renee stepped aside and motioned for him to go in.

Sara sat at the far end of the table, a neat stack of files sitting to her right. She focused on the document directly in front of her. He quietly closed the door behind him, so as not to disturb her, but the click of the door had her looking up. From her expression, he realized he caught her by surprise.

"Sorry. Didn't mean to interrupt you."

She picked up the paper she was working on and slid it into a file folder before she stood. He noticed she wiped her hands on her pants, as if she were nervous about something, before she put her hand out to shake his.

"No, you're fine. Nice to see you again." She gestured to the water bottle in his hand. "I see Renee got you settled."

He nodded at the files.

"Looks like you're keeping busy. Did the newspaper retraction create some of that?"

"In a way." Sara took a seat and Jared followed. "I've got something I want to talk to you about."

He'd planned to hear her out, but the tone of her voice made him uncomfortable. Jared suspected whatever Sara said next was something he didn't want to hear. To change the subject, he reached into his briefcase, pulled out an envelope and slid it to Sara.

"What's this?" Sara asked as she looked down at the envelope. He noticed she didn't pick it up.

"Confirmation that the agreement Doug and Ron signed with Michael is invalid. I made some phone calls. Not everyone has gotten back to me, but from what I've heard so far, there are many more people who will be willing to corroborate the situation."

He watched Sara push the envelope back to him.

"We need to discuss something." She took a deep breath before she said, "I've started looking for a new position."

He blinked a few times while he digested her comment.

"I thought you liked working on the renovation project. It's been a lot of work, and I know I should have mentioned Cynthia's phone calls, but that's no reason to quit."

She pushed her hair behind her ear, distracting him as he wondered if her hair was a soft as it looked.

"I'm not quitting the project. That is unless you want me to. But I do need to leave this firm."

His eyes jerked back to hers.

"Okay, you need to start over and explain what is happening. It's selfish, I know, but I have no desire to find another local counsel. Quite frankly, I wish I could clone you. I could use someone like you in Chicago."

Despite her professional demeanor, the sparkle in her eyes told him she was interested by the idea.

"Are you serious? Because I'd be happy to consider a position in Chicago. But I'm not going to move just for this project. I need a longer-term position."

Excitement, anticipation, and something like trepidation hit him all at once. Sara had been adamant when she took the job she didn't want to move. This was a complete reversal of her earlier position. While it would be challenging to conceal his feelings toward Sara if she were working in Chicago, he needed a talented and strong counterpart.

All of these thoughts swirled through his head when Sara asked, "What do you think?"

To buy himself time, he walked away from her and looked out the window. A yellow-bellied bird looked at him, then tapped on a branch.

"I like the idea, but I'm confused."

"Why?"

Jared turned back to study Sara's face.

"I didn't think you wanted to leave town. With your family here and everything." He walked back to the table and sat down. Clasping his hands together, he continued. "I have to ask. Why the change of heart?"

"Fair question. Professionally, this project has made me realize I am capable of more. I appreciate all that I've learned here, but it is time for me to be more autonomous."

"What about this project? There's still a lot of work to be done."

"Greg's capable of running the show. You just said Michael's not an issue, and I've cleaned up after Cynthia. I can fly back and forth when needed."

She was right. Even if she took over the renovations in other cities, she would have plenty of bandwidth to oversee them all.

Jared asked, "And personally?"

He noticed a slight pause before she spoke.

"Personally, I'm ready for a change." Sara held up a hand as if she knew where Jared's line of questioning was going. "I know Bill and Rich filled you in on my family life. Suffice it to say, this project has taught me I don't need to be local in order to stay connected with my sister and her kids."

"What about your mother? I seem to recall Bill mentioning that she's a thorn in your side."

A hint of a smile crossed her face as she nodded. "That's one way of phrasing it." She sobered up when she asked, "You know, asking me questions about my personal life creates an HR nightmare."

Chuckling, Jared said, "I know. But I need to understand what changed your mind about moving. You are absolutely the right person for Chicago, but I assumed you wouldn't want it. Which goes back to your mother. Does this request have something to do with her?"

"I'd be lying if I said it didn't, but it's more of a perk than a reason." She stared down at her hands for so long Jared wondered if she was going to answer. He knew the minute she sat up taller, she made up her mind. "Yes. I want to start the next part of my professional life without living in the shadow of my mother, wondering what she's saying about me, whether she's going to make my working life difficult." Sara slid her chair out and circled around the table. "I've always been able to stand on my own without her help or assistance, but I need to do it away from here. I'm an excellent attorney, but people don't take me seriously because I'm Helene's daughter. Now I'm ready to take the next step and if that means I have to move, then so be it."

Hearing that, Jared said, "When do you want to leave?"

"How soon do you want me?"

Jared stood up and extended his hand.

"Welcome aboard. Let's get this move started."

37

"We're going to miss you, Aunt Sara. Why do you have to move away?" Libby asked as she snuggled next to Sara on the couch. "Who's going to babysit us when you're gone?"

"Don't give me that. You stay with your grandma and grandpa all the time." Sara rested her head on her niece's. "Besides, when I move, you can come visit me. We can check out the big city on our own. Maybe do some shopping."

"That's not fair. I want to come too. The soccer hall of fame is there," said Blake as he bounced a soccer ball on the floor. "That's way more fun than shopping."

Sara wasn't sure she agreed with Blake, but she was excited to get out of town and be on her own. She still couldn't believe that Jared offered her a job in Chicago, but she wasn't going to question it. A little more space between herself and her family would be nice.

On the other hand, she'd gotten closer to Blake and Libby, and she would miss being in town. Visiting them a couple of times a year and having them come to her would be great, but it would change their relationship. She sighed as she gave Libby a squeeze. She knew what she needed to do, but it hurt, nonetheless.

"Why did you sigh, Aunt Sara?" asked Libby. She should've known Libby was paying attention and would know something was bothering her. "Did we do something wrong?"

"Absolutely not, Libby. You and Blake are fine. I'm just thinking about all the things that have to be done before I leave." Tomorrow was her last day at the office. She had the final checklist of things to do tucked away in her briefcase. Sara pushed herself off the couch and turned back to pull Libby up as well. "Okay, let's go make some cookies. We can wrap some up for Greg to take home when he drops off your mom."

Blake tossed the soccer ball in the basket sitting next to the couch. "Can we do a double batch and give some to Uncle Brad and Uncle Carlton the next time they come over? Uncle Brad really likes chocolate chip cookies."

She nodded, glad to change the subject from her upcoming move.

"To the kitchen!" she called as she led the way.

Two hours later, Sara watched as Libby taped a bow on top of the third plate of cookies. Not only had they baked cookies, Libby plated and decorated each package.

"I think you're watching too many cooking shows, Libs," said Sara as Blake handed her the last mixing bowl to put away. "The cookies are fine on a plate with plastic wrap."

Blake shook his head at Sara.

"Don't get her started on the art of food presentation," said Blake as he tossed the dish towel on the counter. "I'm going to my room. Soccer practice is tomorrow, and I need to get my rest if I'm going to kick Alex's—"

Sara's eyes narrowed as she glared at her nephew.

"Don't even think about it," she said, cutting off his sure-to-be colorful expression. "No foul language in front of me."

"How is ass a bad word? It's in the Bible."

Before she could respond, Blake ran out of the room.

"He does that to Mommy all the time," said Libby. "She says it's because he's a boy and boys do things to irritate their mothers."

Sara hid her smile from Libby when she thought about all the ways Libby would be irritating her mother in the upcoming years. Puberty and teenagers promised to challenge Tasha, which was another thing that Sara would miss. Though she was sure to hear about it!

"Go ahead and get ready for bed, too. Do you want me to come read with you?" Libby didn't need anyone to read to her, but Sara still enjoyed sitting in bed next to her niece while the two of them read their own books. "I'm re-reading *Murder on the Orient Express*. The book is still better than the movie."

Sara saw a spark in Libby's eyes. "Maybe I could read to you. Ms. Jones assigned me *Mrs. Frisby and the Rats of NIMH*. Mommy lets me read out loud to make it more entertaining."

"Of course, you can read to me," she said as she gave Libby a quick hug.

With newfound excitement, Libby scurried out of the kitchen. "Thank you, Aunt Sara. I'll meet you in my bedroom."

Wiping a few leftover crumbs from the counter, Sara grabbed a glass from the cabinet and poured herself some water. She leaned back and looked around the kitchen. Tonight had reminded her how much she loved hanging out with her niece and nephew and how much she would miss them when she moved. Frequent visits would keep her connected, but the kids would get more involved with school and sports and friends in the upcoming years.

"It's still the right thing," she said to the empty kitchen. Finishing off her water, she put the glass in the dishwasher and turned off the lights. She wanted to make the most of her time with the kids before she left.

"Sara." She felt someone tug on her arm, but Sara rolled away from the touch. The tugging turned to poking. "Sara, wake up!"

Sara struggled to go back to sleep when suddenly she remembered. She was babysitting! Her eyes flew open, and she realized she was lying next to Libby in her niece's bed, the book they were reading tucked between them. Her sister stood over her, a huge grin on her face.

"Rats put you to sleep, too?" Tasha whispered, picking up the book.

Blinking to clear the sleep from her eyes, Sara gently scooted off the bed and bent down to kiss her sleeping niece's forehead. She tiptoed out of the room, waiting in the hallway while Tasha turned off the lights and quietly closed the door.

"I usually do okay, but Libby wanted to snuggle in bed while she read. Blake fell asleep early, so I didn't think it would hurt."

They walked into the living room, and Sara looked around.

"Where's Greg?"

Her sister gave her a thoughtful look and said, "His boss's last day is tomorrow so he went home to get some last-minute work done for her. Seems she's leaving him without a lot of notice."

Sara stretched her arms over her head and yawned.

"He had two weeks. He'll be fine. I, on the other hand, have to pack the last of my stuff tomorrow. That could be brutal."

Tasha rolled her eyes.

"Cry me a river. I bet all you have to do is put a few knick-knacks in a box and you're finished."

Knowing her sister was right, Sara countered, "Hey, I have more than that. Renee and I are meeting with the relationship coordinator." The receptionist had been thrilled at the prospect of dating help. "Thomas wouldn't transfer the package until we both met with him."

"That was a nice thing you did for Renee. She deserves it," said Tasha. "I just hope he can find her someone suitable. I'd hate for her to get all excited then not find a good match out of things."

"Thomas has some good ideas." Switching subjects, Sara asked, "Did Brad tell you he and Carlton are coming to Chicago next month? They felt bad they wouldn't be here to say goodbye, but I told them it was okay. It's not every day you get to meet your surrogate."

"Brad was so giddy he had a hard time talking on the phone. I'm happy for them. But the thought of having more babies? Not for me."

Picking up her purse, Sara turned back to her sister.

"I thought Greg wanted kids of his own?"

Tasha shook her head. "We talked about it. As far as he's concerned, Blake and Libby are his. He wants to adopt them after we get married." A frown darkened her sister's face as she continued, "That'll depend on Doug, but that's not something I'm dwelling on right now." As if to prove she wouldn't be bothered by her ex-husband, Tasha flashed her diamond solitaire at her sister and gave a mischievous smile. "Did I mention I'm engaged?"

"Only every five minutes."

An awkward pause arose between the sisters, and Sara felt her shoulders tighten.

"Have you said goodbye to Dad?"

Relieved she didn't have to answer questions about Helene, Sara relaxed a little. "We met for lunch yesterday. He's planning to come out to Chicago in a couple of months. Just to make sure I'm settled."

"Maybe by then, Mom will have come to her senses."

Sara glanced at her watch to avoid her sister's gaze. Both of them knew it wasn't going to happen, but for some reason Tasha retained her optimism. Rather than squash her sister's hope, Sara said, "I need to head out."

"Okay. I'll walk you to the door."

Sara dreaded this moment all week. As excited as she was to start over some place new, she was going to miss her sister.

Dropping her purse to the floor, Sara enveloped her sister in a hug. Tasha squeezed her back.

"Maybe I'll move to Chicago too." Tasha stepped back and wiped a tear away from her eye. "Then you could babysit the kids all time."

Sara retrieved her purse and grabbed the doorknob.

"That's assuming I don't meet the man of my dreams, fall madly in love, and move to some island somewhere." It crossed her mind that Jared might like a tropical beach, but she pushed the thought away. This move to Chicago was a new start for her career, not for her love life. Opening the door, Sara leaned back for another quick hug, then started down the porch steps.

"Call me when you get there," Tasha said as she leaned against the door frame. "Good luck with the drive. Love you!"

"Love you, too!"

As Sara walked to her car, she pushed aside the sadness she felt and focused on the excitement of the move. She slid into her car, started it, and backed out of the drive. Glancing at her sister's house, Sara knew she made the best decision she could make. For herself this time. Which was all that mattered.

DID YOU LIKE IT?

If you enjoyed *My Best Decision - Sara's Story*, please leave a review. Reviews are wildly important for authors. Word of mouth is what sells books and lets authors continue to tell their stories. Thanks for your support!

ABOUT THE AUTHOR

Carole Wolfe started telling stories in the third grade and hasn't stopped since. While she no longer illustrates her stories with crayon, Carole still uses her words to help readers escape the daily hiccups of life.

When Carole isn't writing, she is a stay-at-home mom to three busy kiddos, a traveling husband and a dog who thinks she is a cat. Carole enjoys running at a leisurely pace, crocheting baby blankets for charity and drinking wine when she can find the time. She and her family live in Texas.

Follow Carole at www.carolewolfe.com.

ALSO BY CAROLE WOLFE

My Best Series

My Best Mistake - Tasha's Story

Made in United States
Orlando, FL
27 June 2022